Aloha Alliance

by

Kate Randle

Contact Information: info@thewildrosepress.com
Cover Art by *Kristian Norris*

The Wild Rose Press, Inc.
PO Box 708
Adams Basin, NY 14410-0708
Visit us at www.thewildrosepress.com

Publishing History
First Edition, 2022
Trade Paperback ISBN 978-1-5092-4388-4
Digital ISBN 978-1-5092-4389-1

Published in the United States of America

Dedication

I dedicate this novel to my hero of a husband, Jason, who always believes in me, my two loving children, Ethan and Violet, and my sister Krista. And to Rachel, the best critique partner and writing friend a girl could ever ask for. Also to my editor Kaycee John. Thank you for helping me to make this novel come to life. Finally, this novel is dedicated to my late Aunt Helen. I wish I could send a copy to her in heaven.

Chapter One

Abigail Hastings fought off a shiver of dread as she pulled her rental car up the long and winding paved drive lined with tall palm trees swaying in the wild wind. After almost twelve long hours of traveling, she was here in Hawaii. But it wasn't the utopia everyone thought it to be. Not by a long shot.

She was so close to the truth she sought and yet still so far away. As she jammed the gear shift into park out front of a gray stucco beachfront cottage, she gave herself a moment to collect her thoughts. Closing her eyes, she heard the ocean waves kicking up a frenzy in the near distance, and she breathed in a deep breath of the crisp salty air. A storm brewed on the horizon. She just hoped she could locate what she needed before the skies opened up and poured down rivers of tears upon her. In her haste to get here, she'd forgotten an umbrella.

Although most people thought of Honolulu as paradise, today's weather begged to differ. And it certainly hadn't been paradise for her late brother, Isaac. Her eyes snapped open as the sole reason for being here hit her like a ton of bricks. She needed to solve his decade-old cold-case murder.

Starting this quest at Jacob Devereaux's house was a logical first step. She was confident he'd written her a threatening letter to try and scare her off. When she'd picked up her rental car at the airport an hour ago, a nasty note had been attached to her dashboard. She turned the words over in her mind as she switched the engine off. No longer having the paper didn't matter. Her eidetic memory served her well. Picturing the paper in her mind, she reviewed the scribbled scrawl.

Go home.
You won't find answers here, only trouble
If you don't leave now!

Such tactics had never been his style, but who else could it have been? No one knew she was coming, not even herself, until a few days ago. She hadn't told anyone.

Nevertheless, she wouldn't be frightened away by a piece of paper with some words scratched on it. If something as trivial as that turned her off, she'd never have become the successful investigative journalist she was today. Jacob had the answers she needed and would give her information, whether he liked it or not. He owed her and this was a favor she hadn't forgotten.

Abigail shook her head and propped her no-longer-needed sunglasses up onto her hair. She exited her rented cherry-red sports car and made her way to the porch with its elaborate glass door decorated with etched leaves, surrounded by a cedar wood frame. As she rang the bell, she shielded her eyes from the glare of the clouds and peeked into the clear space between designs in the door.

Stark white yet plush-looking sofas, love seats, and chairs accented with gray pillows filled the space, along with a white wood dining set that seated eight. A marbled gray-and-white floor made the area look like a spread out of a home design magazine. This scene, this house, was so unlike the Jacob she used to know. He didn't care about ornate furnishings or lavish finishes.

But then, she didn't know him anymore. Not really. Not like she had so long ago. In fact, she'd always had a bit of a crush on her brother's best friend way back when. Yet like everything else about him, even that was now a distant memory.

After she wasn't getting an answer after ringing the bell a few times, she knocked on the door. The rapping sound competed with the whistling wind around her but didn't elicit any response. She knocked some more. He was obviously home. She'd deduced that from the fact she'd passed a jet-black SUV at the end of the driveway on her way up here.

Of course, she hadn't called first. She just stuffed his letter in the trash at the rental car parking lot and drove straight to his house. She wasn't sure he would even take her call after all this time. So she just decided to show up. Use the element of surprise to her advantage. It had worked wonders in her five-year career as an investigative journalist.

When people didn't know you were coming, they didn't have time to prepare their lies or stories about whatever you wanted to ask them about. She was quite sure he would never lie to her, but stories were a whole other matter altogether. Besides, a lot of time had passed since she'd been in contact with him, and he'd clearly changed, given the tone of his unsigned note. Abigail tapped her wedge sandaled shoe on the cobblestone walkway and groaned as her maxi dress swirled around her like a whirlwind. No response at the door wasn't factored into her plan.

Everything she'd done over the last decade had

been for the singular fact one day she'd come here to Hawaii to solve Isaac's cold case once and for all. Her brother's death never strayed far from her mind. And here she was. Except she couldn't get the one man who she knew could point her in the right direction to answer his door.

Maybe he was out back. That made more sense. Because although the house didn't fit the lifestyle she'd assumed Jacob had taken up after he'd decided to make the island of Oahu his home, he did love the ocean. And having the ocean in your backyard must be heaven for a surfer. Except he wasn't a surfer anymore, was he?

Not according to the news story she'd come across, which detailed him thwarting the kidnapping plot of a celebrity. He was now the head of some sort of elite police task force that answered only to the governor. When the story had landed on her desk a week ago, she knew it was a sign.

A sign that it was finally time to come to Hawaii and solve the unsolvable murder case that had plagued her for a decade. She had both money and knowledge under her belt; now she just needed a clue. And her brother's best friend was the best place to start. It was obvious he didn't want her here, otherwise, he wouldn't have bothered with the loathsome letter, but she didn't care.

Her brother deserved justice. She was going to make that happen.

Abigail abandoned her knocking and decided to check in the backyard. She rounded the corner of the house and strode across the grass. At the end of the lawn, she came to a few white wooden steps leading down to the beach. She kicked off her sandals and carried them as she descended. Her feet sank into the velvety white sand at the bottom.

She took another step, then froze as the cold barrel of what she could only deduce was a gun pressed against the the back of her skull. As if on cue, the dark skies above opened up with a flash of lightning and a resounding boom of thunder. Rain pelted down around her, soaking her hair and thin dress.

"Hands up and don't move a muscle," shouted a deep masculine voice that was so achingly familiar. It was as if she'd just stepped back in time a full decade. But the gun was new. Uh-oh. Just what had she gotten herself into now?

****

Lt. Jake Devereaux never went anywhere without his handgun. And this was precisely the reason why. He'd just come back from his before-work morning jog on the beach when he heard someone knocking at his front door. When that particular behavior failed, said visitor began ringing his doorbell enough times to wake the dead. Visitors weren't welcome on the best of days. Not that he had many of those anymore.

Visitors or good days. He was "married" to his job, according to his ex-fiancée. And entertaining anyone other than his task force team at his rented beachfront cottage was out of the question. Which left only one thing: the uninvited guest might very well be related to the murder suspect he'd just put behind bars yesterday and had already been granted bail. The man vowed revenge as some of them often did, and even though his address was unlisted, it wasn't impossible to find him. But he was always ready, and today was no exception.

Although, as he pointed his gun at the petite form

in front of him, something in his gut told him this wasn't right. First of all, she was female and not a match for any of the acquaintances he'd investigated in relation to his murder suspect. Also, she didn't look like a criminal, at least from behind. The women he'd put away in his time were few and far between. They also didn't drive fancy sports cars like the one he'd seen as he'd come across the front lawn to follow her path. And they didn't usually ring the doorbell.

Yet he couldn't be too careful. One false move in his business could land him in the hospital. Or the morgue. And until this woman identified herself, his gun would stay put. "I said, put your hands up. And slowly turn around."

The woman's perfectly manicured nails painted a deep purple shot up in front of him, and he backed his gun away ever so slightly to allow her to turn around. Her shimmering bronze skin looked dewy from the falling rain and hinted at the fact she might be a local. Thick ebony hair fell in waves down her back, but he still couldn't place her.

"Okay, okay. I'm sorry," she said. "I shouldn't have snooped. But you didn't answer your door."

The woman wore a sexy black tank-top dress, so she wasn't concealing a firearm, and the sandals in her hand suggested she might be a tourist looking for beach access. Jake made it his business not to make mistakes. Taking another step back, he lowered his gun. "This is private property. If you're looking for the public beach, it's half a mile down the road."

"I wasn't looking for the beach, although it's gorgeous. Minus the rain, of course." The woman twirled and lowered her hands. The fact that her dark eyes and full lips were upturned in a slight smile despite having just had a gun pointed at her struck him. She looked familiar and not, all at the same time. "I was looking for you, Jacob."

She had to be someone from his past. Someone he used to know. And yet he didn't. No one had dared call him by his formal name in years. He didn't know that person anymore. Jacob Devereaux no longer existed. It was Lt. Jake Devereaux now.

She took a step forward. Her smile brightened the dismal dark day. Like a beacon of light guiding him home. Who was this woman?

"It's me, Abigail."

He took a couple more steps back, and then it dawned on him like the sun rising out of the fog. This was his late best friend's, Isaac's, sister. In the ten years that had passed between them without contact, she had grown from an awkward teenager into a beautiful woman.

She was the one he'd spent countless hours teaching mathematics to when all she wanted to do was write stories. The one who his best friend had protected with his life and limb until his dying breath. The woman who he'd called every week after Isaac's death, just to hear her voice and apologize. Until a year later when she'd asked that he never call her again. But now, Abby Hastings stood in front of him.

"Abby?"

She nodded and took a tentative step toward him. "It's Abigail now. And I heard you're Jake now?"

He shoved the gun in the back waistband of his athletic shorts and smoothed down his faded rain-soaked blue T-shirt. He was Jake, all right. Running a hand down his more-than-five-o'clock shadow, he wished he'd at least had the sense to shave before his morning run. Who was he kidding? He wasn't the clean-cut kid she'd known all those years ago. Far from it. Why pretend to be something he wasn't? He'd given up that fruitless habit after his fiancée, Tamara, had left him a year ago.

"Um, yeah. I'm sorry. About the gun. I just don't get a lot of visitors, and when I do, it's never good news." Although he was fairly certain her out-of-the-blue visit wasn't good news either.

"It's okay. Believe it or not, I've had a gun or two pointed at me in my time. And gotten more than a few threatening notes warning me off a case. Did you really think that would work?"

He arched a brow. "What kind of novelist has guns pointed at her on a regular basis, and what's this about a threatening note?"

As he recalled, she had promised to go to school to pursue her passion for creative writing after high school. Although he barely had two dimes to rub together after his surfing career tanked and he decided to go to the police academy, he made sure she had the money for her college education since he knew her mother couldn't afford it.

She laughed. That light, airy sound had always been infectious. And it almost was again. Almost. "I'm not a novelist. That wouldn't pay the bills or help me solve Isaac's murder. I'm an investigative journalist. Ever heard of *Investigative Estate*? I'm their top reporter. And don't pretend you didn't leave a note in my rental car telling me to go home. I'll admit, it's not your usual MO, but then again, a lot has changed in the ten years we haven't seen each other."

He pursed his lips. He'd heard of the show she'd mentioned, but he'd never watched it. His real life was enough of a seat-of-your-pants adrenaline rush, and he didn't need to add sensationalized crime news to the mix. "I didn't leave anything for you. I had no idea you were even coming here. Are you saying someone threatened you? Let me see it."

She waved her hands around as if dismissing his request. "Are you saying you didn't write the note?"

"Yes. That's what I'm saying. And if someone else did, you might be in danger. Did you see anyone following you here?"

She shook her head and pursed her lips. Obviously oblivious to the fact that she might be in real danger. "No. And if they did, they'd be as lost as me. This place wasn't exactly easy to find. Not to mention getting the address in the first place. What kind of lieutenant moves six times in ten years? But wow, I must say. I think you've hit the jackpot with this place. It's gorgeous."

He sighed. "This place isn't mine." He had nothing to show for in his eight years as a cop except for a stellar arrest rate and clocking in more overtime than anyone else on the force. But as for his personal life? Nada. Zip. Not even a permanent residence. "I rent it from some hotshot real estate mogul. It came furnished, which suited me fine, and he likes the idea that someone from law enforcement is watching over his property. Doesn't charge me a lot."

She tilted her head to the side like she always did when she thought too hard. "Are you okay?" She stepped forward and held out her hands to him like she'd done a thousand times when they'd lived back in Michigan, and he'd shown up at their door unannounced after a fight with his dad.

No, he wasn't okay. Hadn't been since the day he lost his best friend, Abby's brother, Isaac. Ten long years had passed, and he still couldn't let it go. His ex-girlfriend had been the one to tell him he'd never find answers. And she was leaving him. Now Isaac's sister shows up out of the blue, and someone is writing notes telling her to leave? "Yeah, of course, I'm okay."

She gave him a knowing look and then stepped forward and took his hands in hers. Emotion welled in his chest, but he stamped it down. Now wasn't the time to get emotional. Never was more like it. He pulled his fingers away before his longing for a past that could never be righted overtook him.

She stepped back and peered over his shoulder into the distance. "It's so beautiful here. I can see why you and Isaac wanted to come to Hawaii. My mother talked about her homeland, endlessly. I don't think she was cut out for life on the mainland. But that's just the way it ended up after she had Isaac and me. I think she thought if she stayed there, my dad would come back. One in a string of many lies she told herself. Drunk or sober. But she was right about how gorgeous it is here. I bet when the sun comes out, it's magnificent."

He nodded. Yet he'd hardly seen the beauty of this place in the last few years. Or the beauty in anything. "Mmm, it is. But I'm sure you didn't fly five thousand miles just to see the view from my rental cottage."

She shook her head and bit her lip. Just like she'd always done when she had to tell him or her brother about something she did that she shouldn't have.

"Spit it out, Abby."

She laughed again. That's what they'd always said. "Okay, Jacob."

"It's Jake, now. I'm not Jacob anymore."

She pursed her lips. "Why?"

"Because…" His voice trailed off. No. He wasn't about to tell his late best friend's sister all of the things that made him turn from the carefree teenager Jacob to the serious workaholic Jake in the last ten years. "Look, it's a long story. One I'm sure you don't have time for in while you're standing in the pouring rain. Just know that I'm Lt. Jake Devereaux now."

Her forehead wrinkled in concentration, and then she gave him a slow nod. "Good. That's good. Because I'm going to need a lieutenant."

Now it was his turn to wrinkle his forehead. "Oh yeah? And why is that?"

"Because I'm here to solve my brother's murder. And you're going to help me."

Chapter Two

If looks could kill, Abigail Hastings would have been struck dead right there outside a rental house on a Honolulu beach. Jacob's dark stare penetrated to her very core, while rainwater tried to drown her. Did he think she was here to soak up the sun and sand?

For some fancy, dancey lieutenant, he wasn't too bright this early in the morning. There was one reason, and one reason only, for her to visit this island, and they both knew it.

One of them wasn't taking it too well.

His stare broke away from her and focused out into the wild surf. After a long moment, he shook his head. "I can't help you. I wish you'd called instead of coming all this way. There's nothing that can be done. Isaac's murder is a cold case, and it will stay cold. I'm sorry. But I will do something about the threats made against you. I need to see that note and try and get forensics to get some prints off of it."

She set her mouth in a grim line and forced herself to look into his bright-blue gaze. If his scruffy clothes and start of a beard were any indication, time had changed him. His dark hair had grown so long he now tied it back from his face, and his skin took on a warm glow like he spent a lot of time in the Hawaiian sun. But his eyes remained the same. Beautiful blue as always.

Looking into them now, she was certain he didn't write those menacing words. "I don't care about the note. It doesn't mean anything. Besides, since I thought you'd written it, I just threw it away in the trash can at the airport. It told me to go home, which I won't. And if I'd called, you wouldn't have had to look me in the eyes and say Isaac's case can't be solved. I'm not about to make it easy on you. I dare you, Jacob now Jake. Say it again. To my face."

She propped her hands on her hips and stared into his blue depths. His gaze caught hers for a fraction of a second, before he looked away. "C'mon. Let's get out of this rain and go get some coffee."

It wasn't the exact answer she wanted, but she'd take it. Caffeine had always helped to solve their problems. And she counted on that to convince him that he needed to help her.

She followed his long strides back from the beach and into the back sliding door of the house. Shaking the sand off her feet, she set her sandals down and looked around. The door entered into the kitchen, and it was bigger than her entire apartment back in New York. Truly magnificent. Oak cupboards lined the walls with sparkling black appliances to match, and oatmeal quartz countertops speckled with ebony finished the space.

He threw her a towel from the stack beside the door, and she caught it, drying off her face and hair. Then she wrapped the fluffy white terry cloth around her middle to help dry off her dress. Jake took a towel and wiped down his face and beard.

"Wow! Look at this kitchen," she said after she'd gotten most of the rainwater off. "You cook?"

He shook his head. "If you mean, do I know how to

13

make coffee, don't you remember my famous lattes?"

"Of course. You still make them?"

He pointed to a state-of-the-art machine in the corner. It's black and chrome gleamed in the morning sunshine, and a grin tugged at her lips. "I may not own the house, but I do own the best latte maker in all of Hawaii. I couldn't get my butt out of bed without it. You want one?"

She yawned in response. It would delay sleep if she indulged, but she wanted some caffeine. "Yes, please."

For the first time since she'd arrived at his place, his blue eyes lit up with a radiance she hadn't been sure he still possessed. Until now.

"Good. Go make yourself comfortable on the porch, and I'll bring it out to you. It's straight through there." He pointed at a hallway through the kitchen.

"Thank you."

He shook his head. "Don't thank me. All you're getting is coffee, only because you came all this way."

Oh, she was going to get a lot more. He just didn't know it yet. She nodded in response and wandered off in the direction he had pointed her in.

The open-air porch was even more spectacular than the kitchen. Sand-colored wicker furniture of every shape and size filled the tiled space along with matching end and coffee tables. With plush ivory cushions on every surface, she didn't know where to sit down first. She peered into the distance, and the view almost took her breath clear away. The rain was short-lived as the sun peeked through the receding clouds. The blue ocean framed the horizon, and the bright-green grassy lawn filled with palm trees and sweet tropical blooms in every color of the rainbow completed this picture postcard scene. She took in a deep lungful of fresh salty sea air mixed with the fragrant flowers.

The sandy beach seemed to stretch for miles in the distance, and the turquoise water with its gentle waves rolling onto the shore transported her into a different time, a different place. This might very well be the paradise her mother spoke of after all.

Closing her eyes, she heard the ocean waves in the near distance. The heated rays of the morning overhead sun in a suddenly cloudless blue sky warmed her skin and bathed her in a glow that almost erased her unwelcoming start to this trip. Besides, she rarely experienced such beautiful weather. Until last night, when she hopped on a red-eye flight, she'd been smack dab in the middle of one of the coldest winters on record in her now native New York City.

Why on earth did she live in a busy, crazy concrete jungle like New York? Because that's where she built her life and career. She wasn't going to go about getting attached to this place just because the sun decided to show itself. No. She came here to solve a murder. Nothing else.

She chose a love seat facing the ocean, and as she sank down in it, the comfortable cushion enveloped her. She leaned forward on the coffee table and picked up a black-rimmed photo frame. It was the only personal picture she'd seen in the entire house and gazing at it made her dry eyes fill with tears.

It had been taken on the day before Jacob and Isaac left for Hawaii. Three smiling faces shone back at her in the photo. A younger Abby with shorter hair smiled a wide grin at being sandwiched between the two equally smiling faces of Isaac and Jacob. Isaac's dark Hawaiian looks so similar to Abby's were in sharp contrast to blue-eyed Jacob. But even still, they looked like a family.

Gazing at the photo instantly transformed her into a child of about twelve again and ready for a splendid day at the beach with her favorite brother. Her only brother. Except he wasn't just her brother. Isaac had been her mother, father, brother, and best friend all rolled into one. And Jacob hadn't been far behind him, even though he wasn't blood.

Those two were the only ones who'd ever cared for her. Her mother tried but just didn't have it in her. Abby had been content for her big brother to watch out for her. Until Isaac and Jacob had gotten the irresistible itch to try and make it big as surfers in Hawaii. Isaac promised to send for her in six months after they'd gotten settled, and she'd finished high school, only that never happened. He died a month before she graduated.

In the photo, they looked like they belonged together and had a bright future ahead of them. At least that's what she'd thought when they snapped the picture on their last trip to the beach in Michigan together. But how wrong she had been.

She set down the photo and swiped at her eyes. There was no sense crying now. She'd cried enough tears over the past decade about this to last a lifetime. Focusing on the ocean waves in the distance, she let the calmness of the ocean wash over her. Her life was in New York now. Alone. If her mother and her absentee father taught her anything, it was she never wanted to have a relationship or get married.

But right now, she couldn't help but be just a little

bit entranced with her surroundings and all of the memories that came with it. She closed her eyes and bowed her head. When she opened her eyes a moment later, Jacob stood over her, tray in hand, and a mournful look on his face.

She stood up and took the tray from his grasp, setting it on the glass table.

"Here's your coffee," he said. "And I brought you some breakfast in case you haven't eaten."

He handed her a steaming mug, then selected the second one for himself as he took a seat on the sofa across from her. "So tell me about you. An investigative journalist? What happened to becoming a novelist? That was your passion."

She nodded. "Yes. At least until Isaac died. But creative writing wasn't going to help me find out who killed my brother. But investigative reporting for a national television show? Let's just say I've learned a thing or two."

And she had. The plan she'd been honing for ten years since the murder was finally coming to pass. Every day and every night, as she finished high school, went to journalism college, and worked her way up the ladder at *Investigative Estate*, solving this case had been her ultimate goal.

"So I guess you don't live in Michigan anymore."

"Nope. I left Michigan after college when my mom died six years ago. No sense in staying there anymore. I headed off to the Big Apple."

"Wait. What? Akela passed away?"

She shrugged. "She was an alcoholic until the day she died. The doctors told her to stop drinking after they diagnosed her with liver cancer, but she never did kick the habit. I mean, she tried as a mother. In her own way. And I took care of her the best I could while juggling school and work after you and Isaac left."

She paused before she continued. "My mother always dreamed about coming back to her homeland, but after Dad left us, she had trouble affording groceries on her waitress salary, let alone a plane ticket here. I always thought it was strange that Isaac and I were half Hawaiian, and we'd never even been to the island. And anyway, she never kept in touch with our relatives, and I don't even know them. I brought her and my brother's ashes with me to scatter on the ocean. I'll do that once the murder has been solved."

He reached across the table and took her hand in his. "I'm sorry. You should have called me. I'd have come to the funeral."

Tears pricked the backs of her eyes, but she fought them back. She hadn't cried over her mother or her death, and she wasn't about to start now. Even if holding his hand stirred something in her she hadn't felt before. It somehow felt…right. She pulled away and felt the loss of his warmth. "We didn't have a funeral. There wasn't anyone to say goodbye, except me. I just had her cremated, and then I left. Don't worry about it. There was nothing you could have done."

He cocked his head at her. "Are you sure?"

She offered a wobbly nod. "Yes, I'm sure."

"Okay." He'd caught on to the fact the conversation about her mother was over. Good. "So you went to New York, huh? Became a famous crime reporter?" He buttered a piece of toast from the tray and handed it to her on a plate.

She smiled. Then took a bite of the bread. The

warm sweet taste of the delicacy mixed with the salty butter was like a yin and yang for her taste buds. That and the fact she hadn't eaten anything except a stale veggie sandwich on the flight over made this like pure heaven. "Is that guava Hawaiian sweet bread?"

"I get it every week from the local market."

She took another bite and reveled in it. "I love this bread. Mom used to make it on the rare occasions she felt like mothering. This is so good. How did you remember I liked this?"

He smiled over. But his smile was laced with sadness. "I remember everything about you. It was you who asked me not to call again, remember?"

She nodded, and sorrow threatened to close up her throat. "Yes. About that—"

He held up a hand. "Water under the bridge. I shouldn't have brought it up. Especially when you're enjoying breakfast. C'mon. Tell me about New York."

She let out a long and slow breath. What could she say about the city she loved? The cheesecake, maybe? "It's busy. Crowded. I work a lot of hours."

He narrowed his eyes. "That sounds awful. Why would you want to do that?"

"Because I do a lot of good for people. We solve unsolvable crimes. And now I'm ready to solve Isaac's murder. Will you help me, Jacob?"

****

There was his formal name again. But the way she said it washed over him like a soothing balm to his battered soul. Not like the way his ex-fiancée spat it out during a fight like she was chewing on rough sandpaper.

But even though he liked having her here, she

wasn't here to stay, not to mention she was his best friend's little sister. Albeit all grown up. But women were off his radar. Permanently. Besides, if she ever found out what he did after the murder, she'd never want to see him again. He'd refused to help her, which he had to, she'd leave, and he'd probably never hear from her again.

"I can't. I wish I could. But trust me. There isn't even a cold case to speak of. As soon as I became a police officer eight years ago, I poured over the case. Read every piece of paper and studied every piece of evidence the police gathered. And I got nowhere. Zip. Zero. There is no case. Cold or otherwise."

Abby put down her bread. "So you gave up? Just like that?"

Heat rose in his cheeks as he recalled studying the case over and over every night for five years. "No, I looked into the case for a long time. No new evidence turned up. Isaac was murdered at the Hawaiian Oasis Resort, where we both worked as surfing instructors, and nobody saw anything. He was beaten up outside the disco around midnight and his body dumped in the alley behind the club. I talked to everyone. Multiple times. So many times, in fact, that I almost got banned from the property. I drove myself half insane because I wanted to solve this case. But I couldn't then, and I can't now."

She shrugged. "You look like you're doing okay. Nice place. A fancy job working for the governor. She's quite a powerhouse, isn't she? I've heard more than a few stories about Melinda Ayoshi. She built her career from the ground up. A stay-at-home mom who became a lawyer, then governor. Impressive."

He smiled. She'd always looked at the bright side of everything. He supposed that had changed now that she'd become a crime reporter. A little part of him hoped it hadn't completely eradicated her innocence. It was one of the things he'd loved about her. "Yes. She's a fantastic boss. So you've been keeping tabs on me, huh?"

She smiled back. "Not at first. But a story came across my desk about you and your team foiling the kidnapping attempt of a celebrity. I thought it was impressive, and I looked you up. And here I am."

"Here you are."

When he'd finally given up on Isaac's murder two years ago, and the governor had invited him onto her elite task force, his life slowly came back to him. He was back on his feet because of his boss and the solid members of his team: Benny Iona, Grace Emery, and Kai Bane. Yet he feared if he ever looked into this case again, he'd be right back where he started. But Abby didn't need to know all that. "Yeah. We do well. It's a good career."

She nodded. "Sounds like it."

His pet cat, Leo, took that opportunity to saunter into the room. Probably looking for a bite of sweet bread. He needed to stop feeding him so much. The last time he'd taken him to the vet, his furry friend was deemed overweight.

The onyx-black creature purred and jumped up onto the couch beside Abby. "Oh, he's so cute," she exclaimed as she stroked him, and he nestled into a comfortable spot, eyeing the treats on the table.

He nodded. "He was a stray I found wandering on the beach one day after I surfed. He followed me home and never left. But be forewarned. He does like sweets, so keep your bread away from him."

She laughed. "Sweetbread? No. Next, you are going to tell me he likes to swim."

She took a piece and offered him a nibble. Leo gobbled it up and licked her fingers.

"Actually, he follows me to the beach most mornings. Guess he's a purebred Hawaiian."

"Yeah. I guess he is. Just like Isaac and me." She stroked the cat some more, and satisfied after his treat, Leo closed his eyes and continued to purr. She turned back to him.

He grimaced. "Trust me. I've been over the case a million times. The police notes and coroner's report, the witness statements and forensic reports, as well as the crime scene photos." The last one was by far the hardest, and he would never get over seeing those until his dying day. Isaac's sister couldn't be exposed to that. He wouldn't allow it. "There's nothing there. No leads. Nothing but a dead end."

She frowned. "Look. I've heard the same thing so many times over the years when we dig up a cold case. And guess what? There's always another angle. Something someone didn't think of that can break a case wide open. One time, all my team and I had to go on to solve a case was a ninety-year-old witness and a bloody sock. I've done it before. And I'm going to do it again. With my brother's case. He deserves justice just like everybody else."

Her plea tugged at his heartstrings. But he still couldn't, wouldn't help her.

He let out a long sigh. "Yes, he does. More than everybody else, I'd say. But listen. If your brother were here, he'd want me to tell you this. Don't do this. Don't open this Pandora's box. It will sweep you away with the ocean tide, and you'll get so caught up in it you won't know what's happening until you're drowning. Look, you've got a great career for yourself, a life in New York as a hotshot reporter. Not too shabby for a girl from Ludington, Michigan. Don't ruin everything you've worked so hard for by going down this path."

She cocked her head at him. "You sound like you're speaking from experience."

He gave her a solemn nod. "I am. Don't do this to yourself. Besides, if someone left you that note, it means they don't want you looking into the case. It could be mob or drug related. I don't know exactly what Isaac was into at the time of his death. He was very distant in the last few weeks of his life. I felt like he might have been hiding something from me, but I never found out what. The best thing you can do is go back to your life in New York, today."

He watched a tear roll down one cheek. She swiped it away with an angry fist. "I have to solve this case."

"Why?" He knew the answer to that question. It was the same reason he'd turned his life upside down and inside out for so long. But he didn't want that for her. She deserved better.

"That's what my brother would do for me. Do you think he'd let a killer go free that had murdered me in cold blood just because he got some scribbled note? No. That's why I vowed on the day he died I would never rest until his case was solved. It's the reason I went to journalism school, moved to New York, and got a job at *Investigative Estate*. I didn't build this life for me. I built it for him. I can't rest and be at peace until I know his killer is caught. Peace is what I need right now."

They all needed, deserved peace, but he knew in his heart even if they caught Isaac's murderer, that wouldn't fill the void that was left by his best friend and her brother. She was searching for something that could never be found.

"You can have peace without going down this road. You've got your whole life ahead of you. Is there someone special, back in New York?" The mere thought of her having a boyfriend or fiancé filled him with unease. Isaac had always said no one was good enough for his little sister. That must be it.

She shook her head. "No, there isn't. And look at you. Acting like you're a million years older than me. There are only four years between us. And since you asked me, I'll ask you. Is there a Mrs. Devereaux?"

He blew out a long breath. There almost was. But it didn't work out. And he only had himself to blame. "No, there isn't. Please say you won't pursue this case. It can only lead to heartbreak and could be dangerous. And I know better than anyone else how heartbroken you were when you lost him."

She pursed her lips. "So that's it? You're not going to help me? C'mon, at least throw me a crumb. Tell me where to start."

"There isn't a crumb to throw. I've been over it. The case is closed." He muttered a small message under his breath that Abby would listen to his advice, just this once. Because if she didn't, the consequences as he saw it were more terrifying than anything he'd encountered in his eight years as a police officer.

For her and for him.

Chapter Three

"Are you ready for this?"

The cameraman gave her the thumbs up, and Abigail ran a hand down her navy jacket and matching pencil skirt. She took the microphone from the second of a two-person crew she'd hired on the fly last night when her plan for Jacob to point her in the right direction of Isaac's murder didn't exactly go as planned. He'd fed her coffee and sweet bread and then asked her to get on the next flight home. She'd told him she would and had even driven back to the airport and changed her return ticket, but in the end, she couldn't get on a plane to New York. Not until her brother's murder was solved.

So she did the next best thing. She booked a room at the Hawaiian Oasis Resort and got some much-needed shut-eye. Then she called *Investigative Estate* and asked if they would support her doing an on-location report to uncover the cold case murder of her only sibling instead of the month-long vacation she'd told them she wanted.

That move was a resounding success and offered her the protection of the network she hoped might ward off any more threats. So here she was. Surrounded by palm trees once again. Only this time, she stood outside the front door of the Honolulu Police Department Headquarters preparing to speak to her viewers.

She cleared her throat and stared straight into the camera. The man did a countdown with his fingers to one; a flashing red light beamed on, signaling there was no turning back. Not this time. "Good morning, and welcome to this special edition of *Investigative Estate*. I'm Abigail Hastings. Today we are on location in Honolulu, Hawaii, and trying to uncover some information about a cold case that has a personal connection for me. My brother, Isaac Hastings, was murdered on the island ten years ago this month. The crime has never been solved. I'm here to get some answers not only for our viewers but for my family."

The fact that she didn't exactly have a family anymore wasn't lost on her, but it was a small detail she decided the public didn't need to know. The cameraman nodded and switched off the camera. "That was great, Ms. Hastings. Good lighting, nice clear voice. Do you want to see the playback?"

She shook her head. The lighting had to be good. It was another beautiful day in Hawaii. Although today, she wasn't barefoot by the ocean, and instead she was dressed in her work clothes. Ready to solve her brother's death, the only way she knew how. By putting it on television.

She was nothing if not determined. "I'm sure it's fine, thank you. I'll double-check it later." She didn't want to stand out here in the bright sunshine much longer in these heavy clothes. Now she understood why everyone dressed casually around here. It was just too balmy for wool and nylon stockings with stiletto heels. Well, no matter. After she got the files, she'd take them back to the hotel and change before she went over them and recorded more footage. She nodded to the cameraman and his crew member. "Now, let's head inside and be ready to roll when we ask for the files."

The man gave her a wide smile. "Whatever you say, Ms. Hastings." The kindness of the Hawaiian people was so refreshing. It reminded her of her mother when she was lucid. Friendly. Easygoing. Like everything she said and did mattered. Something she'd rarely experienced in her childhood and even less so as she climbed the ladder in the cutthroat world of investigative reporting. Of course, Isaac and Jacob had always made her feel that way.

All that was in the past.

She traipsed up the concrete steps with a steady staccato beat as the cameraman and his young son trailed behind her. The two-man team were perfect for her. They knew the island inside out and had promised to follow her wherever her story might lead. When she pushed open one of the double glass doors, she was hit with a wave of cool air. Breathing a sigh of relief from the oppressive heat outside or was it the oppressive words she had to speak, she stepped farther inside the building.

The dull beige tile floor and drab gray walls were the first place she'd seen here that was absent of vibrance and color like the rest of the island. It was what she was used to, back home in New York, and it was oddly comforting. Everything had seemed foreign when she'd stepped off the plane. Hawaii was a place of serenity and light. Even the airport had a relaxing island vibe. But the police station? Not so much. But that was okay. A bit of normalcy was in order.

Abby motioned for the camera crew to follow her up to a window which held a round gray microphone in the center so she could be heard through the glass. An officer in a black polo shirt with a badge attached to one hip and a gun on the other approached just as she waved to the cameraman to roll.

"Can I help you, ma'am?" He had a shaved head and a warm, friendly expression. His kind dark eyes hinted at the fact he was always on alert.

"Yes, please." She straightened her shoulders and met the man's gaze. "I'm here to retrieve all of the public files available on a murder from ten years ago. Isaac Hastings is the name of the victim. I'm prepared to file any papers necessary to obtain this information."

The officer smiled. "Thank you, ma'am. Let me look into that for you. Please, have a seat over there, and someone will be with you shortly."

The policeman pointed to a row of white metal chairs and two vending machines along a wall in the far corner as she blew out a breath. She could be waiting here for hours, days even. Her previous investigations had taught her that hard lesson. She'd hoped a wide grin and a camera crew would speed up the process in paradise. No such luck. "Okay. Thank you."

She signaled to the cameraman to turn off the camera, then stomped to the empty row of chairs. With no one else in the station this early Tuesday morning. She wouldn't have to wait too long. Would she?

Three hours and two black coffees from the vending machine later, she was still seated on the metal chairs. Waiting and then waiting some more. She'd gone up to the window several times to check on the status of her request. The police personnel and clerks behind the counter were always polite, but they always had the same answer. Take a seat and wait.

She'd sent the camera crew home an hour ago, and her patience was wearing less than thin at this point. As she stood and prepared to go up to the counter one more time, the door to her right flew open, and in strode Lt. Jake Devereaux.

Dark glasses shaded his eyes, and he'd swapped his beachwear of yesterday for a button-down white shirt and khaki suit. The handgun he'd pointed at her yesterday was attached to his hip in a holster along with an official-looking shield. He'd cut his hair short which matched his curt nod. She was sure he was rolling those brilliant blue eyes underneath his shades.

"Sit," he barked over at her like she was some sort of misbehaving puppy, and then he lumbered over to a door beside the glassed wall office.

Um, no, she'd stand, thank you very much. She watched as he punched in a key code on the door and then disappeared through the door only to reappear a moment later behind the glass. He made his way over to the police officer she'd been hounding for half the morning and slapped him on the shoulder.

Great, that was just great. They knew each other. That much was obvious. The man slapped him back, and they shook hands. Then he leaned over toward Jacob. She took a few steps closer to see if she could hear anything, but the only sound in the air was her heels clicking on the tile. If only she could click her heels and transport herself right out of this mess.

Getting her hands on the files was hard enough. She didn't need Lt. Jake making it even harder with his connections all over the island. It was why she'd wanted his help in the first place, but when he'd refused, she realized she was on her own. Now what?

Maybe she should leave. Try and get the information from one of her sources that she sometimes used for her crime reports back in New York. She pulled her smartphone out of her jacket pocket and glanced at the time. It was almost eleven in the morning here, which made it five in the evening in New York. If she hurried, she could catch someone at the office and have some useful leads in her hands by tomorrow.

Yes. That would be a much better use of her time than another run-in with the wall he had put up around the case. And himself. It had been so refreshing to see him again yesterday and catch up after all this time. She'd enjoyed talking with him more than she'd imagined—until he'd flat-out refused to help, then sent her on her way.

So now, it was as if his warm smile of yesterday had been a figment of her imagination. He'd made it clear last night he wanted her out of Hawaii. Well, she wasn't going to do that. But she could definitely put some space between them. She walked back over to the chairs and picked up her purse and laptop bag. Then she scrolled through her messages as she made her way to the exit.

A door slammed behind her before she could reach the exit. "Abigail, wait. Where do you think you're going?"

She turned at the voice and the use of her full name. He really wasn't happy with her if he wasn't calling her Abby, but come to think of it, she wasn't exactly happy with him either.

She turned and gave him an exaggerated eye roll to indicate she wasn't seventeen anymore and didn't take orders from anyone. "I'm leaving. Obviously, I'm not going to get the files now that you're here. I thought you wanted to stay as far away from this case as you could. So why are you here?"

He sighed and propped his glasses up onto his head. His bright-blue gaze bore into her like the endless sky she'd stared into this morning from her balcony at the resort. "I'm here to save you. From yourself."

****

Jake knew from Abby's expression that had been the wrong thing to say. Times infinity wrong. She'd always had a stubborn streak, and it had gotten stronger over the years. Must be the investigative reporter in her.

Even still, she wasn't going to get the files. Not without his help, which he still wasn't ready to give. He'd hoped after they chatted last night, he'd convinced her to go home. She'd said as much, and he took her at her word. But of course, she did the exact opposite of what he'd wanted. Figured.

"I don't need saving. From you or anyone else." She turned and marched away from him.

He caught up with her in a few long strides. Yup, he'd been right. He needed to choose his words more carefully. Something he was quite out of practice with given the fact that the only person he spoke to most of the time was his cat, Leo. And Leo didn't really care what you said, as long as he was well fed. "I know. I didn't mean it like that. It's just…this case will make you crazy. Trust me."

She flashed eyes full of pure fury in his direction and then shook her head. "Don't you get it? Not solving this case is making me crazy. I won't have lasting peace until whoever murdered my brother is caught and punished. And if you're not going to help me, that's

31

fine. But just stay out of my way. Because I'm going to solve this murder, with or without your help."

He was afraid she would say that. Was up half the night thinking about her and making calls to see if anyone saw someone putting a threatening note on her rental car. But it was a dead end. No one had seen anything. This morning, he felt like he'd been run over by a dump truck and planned on taking it easy on his one day off.

He was about to check in with the airport to see if she'd got on a flight last night, but his partner Benny interrupted him with a call from the station. He said the governor had personally asked that if anyone had questions about this case, they should talk to Jake, and a reporter named Abigail Hastings arrived at the station a while ago. The governor knew he had gone over this case inside and out. He owed her for all of her support and for taking him on her elite task force, and he was ready to do anything for her. Anything but this. "Look, let's go get some lunch and talk this over."

She raised a brow. "If by talk, you mean you're going to talk me out of this, then no thank you. I will not be talked out of it, and you of all people should understand."

He shook his head. "I'm not trying to talk you out of it. Not anymore." The little white lie left his lips before he could stop it. She was definitely wearing him down. But would he cave? Should he?

"Prove it."

He held up a finger to her and then jogged over to the door that led to the inner office. Punching in his code, he opened the door and grabbed one of the boxes on the table. His partner, Benny, glanced up. "You okay, Jake? You want me to help you out with the reporter?"

He smiled at Benny, the one to play practical jokes on the team and the best partner a guy could ask for. They and the other members of his team, Grace and Kai, had been through everything together. Thick and thin since they'd been placed on the governor's task force two years ago. Jake didn't trust a lot of people. But he trusted Benny and the rest of the team. With his life and everything else.

Jake shook his head. "Nah, I got it. She's the victim's sister. We grew up together, back on the mainland."

Benny gave him a slow nod. "Ah, okay. You sure? I heard the gov asked you to take care of it. But I can. You know, you've been doing so great lately at work and with other stuff. I don't want the papers in that box to mess it up for you."

Benny pointed to the cardboard in his hands that he said he'd retrieved from storage "just in case." It would mess up something, all right. And Benny was right. He was finally back on track after his ex-fiancée, Tamara, left him, and he'd finally given up hope of ever solving Isaac's case along with the one thing he'd done that only his partners knew.

Opening up this box could unload a tsunami's worth of guilt and pain, sending him sliding backward into oblivion. But he didn't want to pawn Abby off on anyone else. He had to show her at least one box if it had the slim chance of convincing her there was nowhere to turn in this case.

"No, I'm good. I've got this. Now you get your butt out of here. It's our only day off this week."

Benny grinned. "I came in to collect some reports. And it's your day off too. Don't forget that."

"I won't." He juggled the box and pushed open the door. Partners like Benny were as rare as a blue moon, and he would heed his advice and take some time for himself. After he got Abby on the next plane home. He'd show her a couple of papers in the box and then convince her the case was a dead-end street. All in a day's work, right?

Jake let the door close behind him, and then he made his way back over to Abby. "Here are the files you wanted. Let's have lunch and go over them."

Abby propped her hands on her hips. "Where are the rest of them?"

"The rest of what?" He feigned innocence, but Abby saw right through him. He had never been able to lie to her, even when it was for her own good. Apparently, that hadn't changed.

"The rest of the files? They don't fit in one box. It was a murder. There have to be at least ten boxes."

Twelve, in fact. And he was sure she'd want to see each and every one of them. "There's more. Look, I'll have the rest sent over to your hotel. You did get a room, didn't you?"

She pursed her lips. "I'm at the Hawaiian Oasis Resort, in the Palm Tree Tower. Room Seven Eleven."

Why was she staying at the hotel where the murder took place? Because she was a good reporter and determined to solve the case. Still, he hadn't been to that resort in years. It was a trigger for him. But one he'd have to face to protect Isaac's sister. "Okay. I'll have them sent over there. Let's meet in an hour. At the Beachside Grill. It's the best restaurant in the resort.

Great burgers, fries, and a view of the ocean. We can talk there. Get stuff sorted while we wait for the files. Sound good?"

She nodded. "Yes. Does this mean you'll help me with the case?"

"It means we'll talk about it." And by that, he meant he'd have to come up with something really convincing to say before they met for lunch. Something that could shut this down once and for all so they could both get on with their lives.

She gave him a bright smile that momentarily blindsided him. Her long hair was twisted up in a tight knot, but it only served to highlight the delicate features of her face. Her wide eyes. Her pert nose. Her full lips. Wow. Why had he never seen her before in this light?

"Okay. Great. See you over there." She reached forward and plucked the box out of his hands. "I'll take this with me. Collateral if you will, just to make sure you keep your promise." And with that, she strode away from him before he could even get a word in. But what would he have said if he'd had the chance anyway?

He groaned and looked at his stainless-steel watch that never left his wrist. It had been a gift from Isaac and was probably his most prized possession. He had a twenty-minute drive to come up with something, and one thing was for sure. It better work this time. He strode out of the double doors of the station, still pondering what he'd say to Abby when he heard her scream pierce the bustle of the afternoon street outside.

Chapter Four

After Jake stepped out onto the concrete steps, he was met with a sea of papers littering the steps and an overturned cardboard box. He rushed past the mess, and his gaze shot over to a tall man with a dark baseball cap low on his forehead. His arms wrapped around Abby's waist and neck as he pulled her toward him. She screamed again as the man pulled her away farther and tried to force her into the back seat of a very new, very expensive, dark sedan that idled at the curb.

"Stop! Police!"

The man looked up, but dark glasses shaded his eyes, and he couldn't get a good view. The man was dressed in dark jeans and a faded white T-shirt, nothing that could help identify him.

Jake pulled out his weapon and aimed, grabbing the attention of the would-be attacker for a fraction of a second while Abby bit into the beefy arm around her neck. The man yelped and loosened his grip just enough to allow her duck away.

He got off a clear shot, but it missed, and the bullet ricocheted off the car, causing a crowd of bystanders to stop and stare. A few rushed over to help as Abby fell against the pavement just out of reach of the man. She scrambled up and ran up the steps toward him. He caught her in a protective hug and pushed her behind him as the man neared the vehicle, and seeing he'd been made, ran around the driver's side of the car.

He got another clear shot, and it shattered the window. The crash of splintering glass hitting the pavement in a rain of showers attracted more attention as uniformed police and detectives flooded out of the building, guns drawn and calling into their radios for backup. The perpetrator jumped into the driver's seat and took off roaring down the midday street. Jake wanted to take another shot, but it was too risky with the crowd of civilians gathering around. "Are you okay?" His voice could barely be heard over the roar of squeaking tires and chatter of cops and bystanders. He holstered his weapon and desperately wanted to go after the car, but not if she was hurt or injured.

She heaved, slightly out of breath. "Yes, I'm fine. Go after him."

He took another quick head-to-toe glance at her. Other than her ripped stockings and a scratch from falling onto the pavement, she appeared unharmed. He nodded and barreled down the street. His legs burned as he ran faster than he'd ever done at the academy or on a job. Sweat beaded on his forehead and arms, but he just kept pushing. As he caught up with the car, he managed to catch the last two numbers on the plate.

The car veered around a city trolley, narrowly avoiding a collision, and turned down an empty side street. He continued the chase, and his breath was coming out fast and furious. But he was no match for this high-end vehicle, and the car revved its engine, turned another corner, and disappeared from his sight.

Burning the numbers seven and six into his memory bank, he bent and swore under his breath. He should have been faster, and he should have gotten all of the numbers on the plate. He'd failed the Hastings. Again. His chest heaved as he struggled to catch his breath. As he jogged back to headquarters, an ambulance and fire truck had arrived on the scene, engines roaring and sirens blazing. The calvary was here, but they were too late. Benny ran up. "Hey, you good? Anyone injured?"

He shook his head. "I'm fine. I don't think anyone was hit except the perp's car. I shot the side, and now it has a smashed window. I tried to get off a third shot, but there were too many bystanders, and I didn't want to risk any of them getting hurt. I got the last two numbers on the plate. Where's Abby?"

In the sea of people milling around, police and civilians alike, he didn't spot her. How could he have left her so vulnerable? She'd said she was okay, but he should have stayed with her. What if she was injured? Or worse? Dread flooded his veins as if his blood had turned ice cold.

Benny smiled and slapped him on the shoulder. "It's okay. Relax. The unis are scouring the streets and interviewing witnesses. Your reporter is with Grace Emery. Kai and Grace happened to be in the area when they heard the call."

Jake's wildly beating heart slowed a little, and his blood pressure began to return to normal. She was okay. Benny pointed to the top of the steps. Grace was with her, head bowed and listening to Abby.

He turned back to Benny. "What else do you know?"

His partner pulled out his memo book and read his notes. "Kai is inside working his magic on the computers and trying to trace the car on the surveillance cameras. Grace is talking to Abigail and getting her statement. She's fine. One tough cookie if you ask me. Are you sure she's just a reporter?"

She was much more than that. Even Benny had seen it, and he'd only just met her. "I'm not sure, buddy. But I do know she's my responsibility. And I'm more than a little concerned someone tried to grab her in broad daylight. In front of the police station no less."

Benny nodded. "Yup. Do you think it has anything to do with the case she wanted the files on? Or was it just a random kidnapping ransom of a tourist gone wrong? We've had a few of those lately with the gang activity going on. You have to admit, she was dressed like a tourist in that heavy suit. No local would be caught dead wearing that."

Jake gave him a half shrug. "Good point. I'm not sure what this is all about. But I'm going to find out."

Benny slid the notebook back into his pocket. "I'm sure. If you need anything else, give me a holler."

"I will. Thanks, buddy."

Benny nodded and made his way back up the steps.

Jake strode over to the steps where Grace hovered with Abby, whispering to her as she wrote down what she was saying. She appeared pale and sipped on a bottle of water. A gray blanket one of the paramedics had brought over was wrapped tightly around her despite the heat of the day.

He kneeled down to her level. "Are you sure you're okay?"

She hugged the blanket tighter. "Yeah. Just a little shook up, I guess. A lot has happened to me as a reporter, but I can't say I've ever been important enough to kidnap before." She barked out a dry laugh and then coughed.

He leaned over and put a hand on her shoulder. "Hey. Let's get you checked out. Just in case. Okay?"

She gave him a wobbly nod. "Okay."

He signaled to a female paramedic with long light-brown hair wearing a dark-blue uniform who he knew was kind and gentle. She was training to be a doctor and the best on the island. "Violet, can you check over Abigail for me? I think she might be a little shook up."

The paramedic nodded and rushed over with her medical bag. "Of course. I'd be happy to."

Jake gave Abby's shoulder a squeeze and then stepped away with Grace to give Violet some space. He shook hands with Grace. Dressed in a blue tank top and black shorts, she looked as though she planned to enjoy a day on the beach. Guilt stabbed at him for burdening his team on their only day off this week. "Hey. Thanks for heading right over when you heard the call."

With those bright-hazel eyes and long blond hair tied up in a high ponytail, she looked more like a model than a cop. But looks could be deceiving. And that's what he needed on his team. Grace Emery was a perfect match for various undercover jobs like drug stings and prostitute rings.

"No problem. Always on duty, right?"

Jake nodded as she stood up and took a few steps away from Abby. "Yup. Sorry about that."

"Comes with the territory, LT. I know what I signed up for."

Even still. He pinched the bridge of his nose to stave off a budding headache. "I know, but I appreciate it nevertheless."

She smiled again. "I know you do."

He massaged the back of his neck with one hand. "What did Abby tell you?"

Grace glanced down at her notes. "She didn't get a good look at the perp. She said he might be a local and possibly in his forties. Other than his tall height, we don't have much to go on. The glasses and the ball cap obscured her from getting a good description. But the tattoo he had looked interesting. She said it was on the right side of his neck, looked big and unique. It was black with no color, but definitely some sort of tribal design, and she drew it out for me the best she remembered. She said it had the three initials, but she could only make out the first one, H."

Grace handed over her black leather memo book to Jake, and he studied the drawing. It was an elaborate triangle with lines snaking to and from each corner. The detailed etching of letters curved under the design, and Abby had drawn the one she'd seen. Jake looked up at Grace. "Recognize it?"

Grace pursed her lips. "Nope. I'll run it through the database and see if I get any hits. I'll also get Abigail to do a sketch of the perp with an artist. We'll catch this guy, one way or another."

"Great. Thanks. I owe you one."

She shook her head. "No, you don't."

Jake peered around at the controlled chaos surrounding them. He wanted to go around, see what he could gather, but he needed Abby safe and out of harm's way in order for him to be able to concentrate. He turned back to her. "I hate to ask because I know it's our day off, but can you do me one more favor?"

"Sure."

Her one word made his veins flood with relief. He

could always count on his team. They came into his life in a very dark time and had been there ever since. "After you do the sketch, can you take Abby back to her hotel?"

Grace gave him the thumbs-up sign. "No problem."

Apparently, there was. Abby jerked into a standing position and threw off her blanket. She held her hands on hips as the paramedic backed away. "I'm not going anywhere until this guy is caught, and we can get to the real reason I'm here."

Violet gave him a pointed look as she stepped away from her now angry victim. "She's okay, as you can see," Violet said. "I bandaged her wrists, and all she needs now is a little rest and relaxation."

Jake nodded in Violet's direction. Rest and relaxation were two words he was pretty sure Abby wasn't familiar with. "Thanks, Vi."

The paramedic smiled and waved as she walked back into the direction of the ambulance.

Jake stepped over to her and jammed his hands in his pockets to keep from pulling her into a hug and seeing for himself she was fine. But she was so strong and so brave she probably wouldn't appreciate the gesture. "I think you've put yourself in enough danger for one day. Please, go with a member of my team, Detective Grace Emery. I trust her with my life and yours. I just need to check out a few things, and then I'll meet you back at the hotel."

She held up her hands, and he noticed the bright white bandages on her wrists from where she's fallen onto the pavement as she tried to get away from her attacker. She wasn't as bulletproof as he'd thought.

When she sighed, he saw exhaustion on her face.

Dark circles rimmed her eyes; she rubbed her forearms as if an invisible chill cloaked the warm day. She looked over to where a uniformed officer was picking up the papers from the box she'd dropped when the attacker approached her.

"Okay, I'll go. But I'm taking the box with me."

Jake might have laughed out loud if she hadn't almost been kidnapped right before his eyes. After all that had happened, she was still determined to get her hands on the evidence box. He had to admire that. But did the box have anything to do with the kidnapping?

Dread clogged up his throat, and he struggled to get a breath in. He hadn't been able to save Isaac, but he wasn't going to let anything happen to her. And if he needed a box of evidence to convince her, that's what he would give her.

"Fine. Take it. But you have to listen to Grace. She's a seasoned cop and knows what she's doing."

She gave him a half smile. "I'll see you later, then. Hopefully, with answers about what just happened."

He'd get answers. They just might not be in time for him to meet her at her hotel. "My team and I, as well as the Honolulu Police Department, are doing everything we can to find out what happened. I promise you that."

If he promised more, he was afraid of what the consequences might be.

Chapter Five

Abby moved to lift the lid off the box of evidence, but a sharp knock sounded at her hotel door before she got the top off. Jacob must be here. Only a mere half an hour had passed since Grace had dropped her off. She hadn't even had time to look at the papers she now possessed. She'd only showered and changed, and here he was. Another pound came again before she reached for the door handle. "Just a minute, I'm coming."

"So is Christmas," came a sharp masculine voice from the other side of the door.

She pulled the door open with a flourish as the breeze ruffled her knee-length dress. Jake stood there, balancing two cardboard boxes with a bag of takeout on top. His dark expression softened when he gazed at her, and her heart skipped a beat.

"Um, a little help here," he said as the takeout bag that smelled like fresh-cut fries and burgers slid to the side and threatened to topple over.

"Yes, of course. Sorry." She caught the bag just in time and ushered him inside.

He set the boxes down on the bed and turned to her, a wry grin on his face. "You look much more relaxed."

"I am," she admitted. "Did you find anything out about the mugging this afternoon?"

His solemn look told her everything she needed to

know. "No. The police couldn't locate the would-be kidnapper. Another member of my team Kai tracked him on the cameras until he went into a dead zone, so they lost him. We got a partial plate, and there's damage to the car, so from all that and your description, we will either find him or the car very soon, I promise. I'm going to go over the witness interviews the uniforms are finishing up now. I've got my team and the HPD on it twenty-four seven."

She took a deep breath and let it out long and slow. It wasn't a solved case, not by a long shot, but she was sure Jacob and his task force would do whatever they had to in order to get to the bottom of this.

He peered over her shoulder and gave a low whistle. "Wow. Look at you with the million-dollar view. The beach, Diamond Head? This is fantastic." He strode over to the open balcony door and peered out. "Leave it to you to do Hawaii in style. Not like when Isaac and I first got here. We stayed at the cheapest downtown hostel we could find."

She gave him a solemn nod. "I heard about that place. My brother even sent me some photos. I can't believe you guys stayed there for three whole months. And it is nice to have money now, especially since we grew up so poor. But if I could, I'd trade it all in for just five more minutes with my brother."

"I know. Me too."

He moved away from the window and held out his arms. She stumbled into them and cried on his shoulder for a long moment. This was one of the first times she'd cried over this. She'd always told herself to be strong and tears don't help solve a murder.

But being here with him, someone who cared about

her and her brother as well as the stress from this afternoon, had just made it all bubble to the surface. And when he spoke those tender genuine words, the dam she'd been holding back for a decade collapsed. He held her in a tender embrace, letting her sob and soak his crisp white shirt with tears and mascara.

After a long moment, she pulled away and grabbed a tissue from the nightstand. "I'm sorry. I didn't ask you here so that I'd fall apart on you. I must be such a mess." She dabbed at her eyes and tear-stained cheeks.

He gave her a small smile. "You're not a mess. And you went through a lot today. But you're beautiful. As always."

The way he said those words warmed her heart from the inside out. A flush crawled up her cheeks, and she opened her mouth to say something. Anything. But no words came out. Her heart skipped a beat again. What was it about grown-up masculine Jake that made her heart flutter so wildly? Before she could answer that, he spoke.

"It's okay. Don't be sorry. I know how much Isaac meant to you, and being here, it just brings it all home, doesn't it?"

She managed a wobbly nod. It did indeed. But crying over it wasn't going to solve her brother's murder. Neither were the jumbled thoughts she had about her brother's best friend. "Yeah. I guess it does."

He nodded and handed her another tissue from the desk in the corner. "I almost didn't stay on the island after the murder. Everywhere I went reminded me of Isaac. But I wanted to try and solve the crime, and I knew it was impossible from the mainland, so I dove into the police academy here headfirst. But after, when

I realized his murder case had gone cold, I already had a good job, so I just never left."

She reached out and dabbed at his tear-stained shirt. "I know what you mean. I can't ever see myself leaving New York. It doesn't have bad memories, but it's not what I thought I'd be doing at this stage in my life. But you gotta go where the work is, right?"

"Yup." He cupped his hand around hers and gave it a warm squeeze. "Don't worry about my shirt. There's lots more where this one came from."

She nodded and continued to hold his hand, feeling the warmth of his skin on hers. Abby didn't want to let go. Not yet. But then he pulled away, and the spell was broken.

****

The soft touch of Abby's smooth skin on his rough, calloused hands brought solace and comfort to Jacob in a way he didn't quite understand. And he definitely didn't deserve. His failure to protect his best friend and later his failure to solve the murder was the very reason she came here and possibly the reason she was in danger. She shouldn't be here. And he shouldn't be holding her hand.

He raked a shaky fist through his hair and paced the length of the elegant hotel room, not meeting her gaze. Even though he and Isaac had worked here for five months after they'd arrived in Honolulu, they'd never set foot inside one of these fancy hotel rooms. They could barely afford to eat, let alone stay at the resort. The posh feeling of the room made him jumpy, uneasy. Or was it the fact that he'd just been holding hands with his late best friend's little sister?

"Hungry?"

Her light voice brought him back down to reality. No, he wasn't hungry. But at least if he kept eating, it would keep his hands from wandering because he was sure this time he wouldn't let go. "Starved. I brought us takeout from the Beachside Grill since we never made it there today. How about you?"

He stole a glance in her direction. She looked like a Hawaiian princess in the sand-colored casual dress. It was a far cry from the serious suit she'd donned at the police station, and now her hair fell in waves over her shoulders and back. She looked ready for a day at the beach, not about to pour over a stack of dusty boxes. He wished he could give her what she deserved. But he didn't even know if he could give her what she wanted. He'd failed at solving his best friend's murder in the past, and if he went down this road again, he wasn't sure the outcome would change. But the consequences might be devastating for him and mean the difference between keeping his job and his sanity or going down the rabbit hole of years ago.

"Yes, me too." She tore into the bag, and the mouthwatering smell of crispy fresh French fries wafted into the air.

"Burgers and fries?" she asked as she pulled out one takeout container.

He nodded. "The best portobello mushroom burgers in all of Waikiki. Along with sweet potato fries. And I added two mango lime cheesecakes. Can't have burgers without cheesecake, right?"

She smiled, and his heart lifted for the second time today. She had this effect on him. Yet he had to do this. Give her the perfect lunch and then...then what? Could he convince a seasoned investigative reporter not to look into the murder of her brother and go back to New York? If he couldn't, the alternative was horrifying.

"Right." She popped a fry into her mouth and let out a satisfied sound. "Mmm. These are good."

He reached into the bag and got one for himself. She was right. The fried potatoes were both sweet and salty, with just a hint of nuttiness. Perfect.

"C'mon," she said, grabbing one takeout box for her and handing him the other one. "Let's eat on the balcony and talk strategy."

The fries had distracted her, all right. For half a second. Now it was back to business. So much for light lunch conversation. He followed her out onto the balcony, and they sat in silence for a moment as they each enjoyed the burgers and more fries. He gazed from her to the ocean and back as he tried to decide which was more stunning. But who was he kidding? It was her. By a long shot. But it shouldn't be.

"Are the other files coming? I want to categorize them and make sure all the bases were covered way back when, and then we can devise a method to retrace all the investigator's steps in real time and see what's changed that might break the case wide open."

The other files weren't coming, at least not until he gave the okay. Which he didn't want to do. He'd spoken with the governor on the way over to the hotel, and she'd left the case in his hands to handle. So now, he had carte blanche to do what he wanted, and that was to keep her far away from this case. She had no idea what she was getting into.

He tried another tactic. "I think this idea is more dangerous than I first thought. If the killer is still out there and was the one who tried to grab you today, you could get hurt. Or worse. We need to weigh our options before we jump into this feet first."

"There aren't any options." Her narrowed eyes were full of blazing fury. "Except me solving this murder. I've done it before on *Investigative Estate* with cold cases, and I'll do it again. Besides, Detective Emery told me this could just be a random kidnapping, nothing more. She told me there's been a rash of tourist attacks lately."

"Even if it was random," he countered, "there's still the note left on your car. Someone doesn't want you looking into this case. If you continue to, how can you be sure harm won't come to you this time?"

She shook her head and bit into another fry. "I don't. And neither do you. Would you be doing what you're doing, catching killers and foiling kidnapping attempts, if every five minutes you had to stop and think about the consequences?"

No. He never thought about the consequences. Except on that one fateful day when he hadn't wanted to go to the club with Isaac because he was tired after a long day of teaching surfing. His best friend said he was getting old if he didn't have the energy to grab a drink after work. Jacob laughed, and Isaac headed off to the bar without him. And never came home. The consequences of that haunted him now and would forevermore until he took his dying breath. "It's different for me. It's my job."

She cocked her head. "It's my job too. And our brother. I know you weren't blood, but he loved you like family. We can't let this crime go unpunished. I know you didn't want me to come here. But I'm here now. And in case you haven't noticed, I'm not leaving until I solve this case. I've gotten the go-ahead from the network executives to focus exclusively on this case for the next month. I have a camera crew at the ready, and after I go through the files, I'm going to film a segment telling the viewers what I've learned. I wish I hadn't waited ten years before coming here, but with Mom, school, and getting my career started, time got away from me."

The bite of burger he'd just taken turned to sawdust in his mouth. "Don't you know that if you're all over the news saying you are going to find and punish the killers, they will definitely go after you? And a hoard of police officers might not be there next time to protect you. Why am I just hearing about this now?"

"Because you're too busy telling me to go home. Look—"

He threw his burger aside and rose to pace the length of the balcony. "No, you look. This is already dangerous. And now you've just put a target on your back by going public with this. What were you thinking?"

She rose on her tippy toes to try and match his height but only came up to his shoulder. But her hands propped on her hips signaled she meant business. "I was thinking I want my brother's killer caught. He was beaten to death and left to die in an alley behind the disco on this very resort. And since you don't want to help me, I'm going to have to use the resources of the show to get any headway on this case. I need contacts, leads, and network backing. All of which you don't want to be a part of. A segment is scheduled to air next week. I don't have much time before I have to come up with something."

"What you're going to come up with is trouble. Who knows what or who else will come out of the woodwork if you go through with this? This is a bad idea. Cancel it. Now."

She sat back down. "No. I won't."

Pulling the lid off one of the cheesecakes, she took a huge forkful and shoved it in her mouth. "Thanks for lunch. And the cheesecake. I've tried it all now, and it was delicious. You can go now. Goodbye."

He dropped into the chair beside her and leaned over with his elbows on his knees so he could look her in the eye. "I'm not leaving. Now, you've gone and put yourself in harm's way again. I can't let anything happen to you. It was bad enough your brother died on my watch. I won't have you getting hurt or worse."

She draped a slender arm over his. "Isaac's death wasn't your fault. Let's get whoever did this, once and for all. We deserve justice. All three of us."

He leaned back in his chair and let the sunshine blanket him in warmth. It was as if he took a moment, what happened all of those years ago would vanish. Maybe the three of them would be sitting here today, laughing and enjoying lunch on this balcony.

But that was all a dream—instead, the reality was he was a cop who never solved the murder of his best friend and whose still grieving sister was almost kidnapped today. He had a big decision to make. He just hoped it wasn't the wrong one.

"Okay. I'll help you. On one condition."

****

Abby paused with a forkful of cheesecake halfway to her mouth. His words had come out as a growly whisper, but she was sure she'd heard him right. He

52

was going to help her with the case. "Thank you. You won't regret this. I promise, I'll do most of the work. I'll tell the network you're on board and—"

He patted her shoulder and then extricated himself from her grasp. "I said I would help you. But on one condition."

Ah yes. That little detail. Did he want to be paid? Because she was sure the network would agree. And it made sense to pay a seasoned expert. Maybe he'd even agree to an on-camera interview. "Of course. You want to be paid for your time? I understand. You're a very busy professional. I can talk to the executives—"

He shook his head and stood, pacing the length of the balcony. "No. This isn't about money. If you want my help with this, you're going to have to turn the camera off."

"What?" She'd just gotten a big favor from the network, and now she'd have to back out of it if she wanted his help. It was true she hadn't signed the contract for the case yet, but still. This might ruin her career and her reputation as a journalist. Something she'd worked years of blood, sweat, and tears to establish.

"You heard me. No camera crews. No television show. No media. We do this on our own, on our time. I can't use the governor's resources or funds because cold cases aren't part of her jurisdiction. And to be honest, she wasn't too happy about a mainland reporter looking into this, but I said I'd take care of it. And I will. But it has to be on my terms. If she gets wind of us looking into this by you splashing it all over your fancy show, we won't get anywhere with this, assuming there is a case at all. Take it or leave it. It's your choice."

She took a bite of cheesecake. The delectable blend of mango and lime with rich cheese help to soften the blow of this hard-to-swallow pill. The best chance she had of solving this murder was working with him. It was why she'd gone to his cottage yesterday. He knew the island. He cared about her brother as much as she did. And that was all that mattered.

If her backing out of the contract blew back on her, she'd just have to deal with it. But if she said no and didn't solve the case because of all the red tape in Hawaii, she'd never forgive herself. She needed a conclusion to this part of her life. She needed everlasting peace. No matter what it cost. "Okay. I agree. No camera crews. I'll cancel the whole thing with the network and just book a month's leave. You work as much as you have to and help me in your spare time. It's just you, me, and a cold case murder. Where do we start?"

He let out a long breath. "At the beginning."

Three hours later, the sun sank low in the sky, and the beach crowd was thinning out fast, except for a handful of people getting a surfing lesson down on the beach. Abby watched as the agile older instructor motioned how to react to the waves from the safety of the sand. The two women and three teens popped up and down from their surfboards and bent their knees, waiting to catch a wave. After they'd pored over the first three boxes, she was taking a much-needed break.

They'd included all the witness interviews, the crime scene photos, which he hadn't let her look at, and the coroner's report, which stated Isaac had sustained three broken ribs, a fractured pelvis, and a head injury that had proved fatal. Her heart split near in two at the thought of her only sibling dying alone and in pain. There was nothing she could do about it now except work to catch his killer.

The network wasn't happy when she called to cancel the show, but she'd deal with the fallout when she went back to New York. Right now, the only thing that mattered was the case. Which as it turned out, wasn't going well. They'd turned the boxes inside and out, but it was all information Jacob had been over a thousand times. He didn't have an eidetic memory like her, but it seemed like he'd memorized every piece of paper and could even recite some of the data to her without even reading it. It didn't seem like any new evidence could be found in these boxes. She bowed her head and pushed the negative thoughts from her mind.

They'd only just begun looking at the case. But he was right. A lot of time had passed without any new leads. So it was up to them to find them. Her eyes flashed open as she heard him approaching from behind.

"Okay, great. Thanks a lot, buddy. I owe you one."

He clicked off the line and joined her at the balcony railing. He brought the fresh scent of sea salt and bergamot with him. She took a deep inhalation, despite herself.

"The other boxes will be here tomorrow morning."

"Thanks." Yet her voice held quite a bit less of the enthusiasm she'd had before she'd opened the first box this afternoon.

He took a long breath, let it out long and slow. "It's almost sunset, a perfect time to surf. If you're not a morning person, that is. Back in the day, I surfed at dawn and at dusk and every good wave in between."

She nodded and pointed at the beach. "Yes. There's a lesson going on down there. Is that what you used to do?"

He put up a hand to shield his eyes from the sunshine. "Yup. We did. Me, Isaac, and the governor's son Liko Ayoshi, who was already a local surfing legend, were hired on the same day, and we became fast friends. Five lessons a day, seven days a week if the surf cooperated. And then we still found time to surf on our own. It was a passion."

She gazed over at him. His handsome features basked in fading sunlight, and she noticed his slightly crooked nose, which now made him look more rugged than refined. "Why'd you stop?"

"It wasn't the same. Not without Isaac. Besides, he was the real deal. I think he'd have made it big if he hadn't been killed. He always placed first or second in all the competitions we entered in. Liko went on to win a few big competitions before becoming a lawyer, but we still keep in touch. I think he told his mother about me, and that's when she asked me to be on the task force. I owe the entire family for getting me back on my feet. But as for back then, I was just along for the ride. But what a ride it was."

The surfing instructor stood up and faced them as he showed the newbie surfers what paddling to shore looked like. "It's not too late. Look at that instructor. He's older. But it looks like he knows what he's talking about. Maybe you should take it up again or teach it in your spare time?"

He leaned over the balcony and peered into the distance as if taking her idea seriously. It would be good for him to loosen up a little. She was pretty sure all he did was work. "Are you thinking about getting your old job back?"

She laughed at her own joke but didn't get a response from him. He continued to stare at the gathering on the beach and leaned over even farther. "What is it? Do you want to go down and talk to the instructor? See if they're hiring?"

He turned back to her in a flurry and grabbed her hand and pulled her inside as he broke into a jog. "Wait. What is it? What are you doing?"

"We need to get downstairs. Now. That surfing instructor on the beach was our old boss."

"So?"

"He's the one who found your brother's body."

Chapter Six

Jake and Abby took the stairs two at a time as his thoughts raced back to a decade earlier. Rusty Collins had been the one who had hired Jacob, Isaac, and Liko, or the "trio of tide chasers" as he'd called them back then, to teach surf lessons, and even though he'd been much older than them, he partied like it was 1999 every night.

"Rusty Collins was the surfing instructor," he panted out as he kept up his pace and explained what was going on all at the same time. "He was there on the night Isaac was murdered and discovered his body. Of course, the police interviewed him, and I've gone over the notes a million times, but when I tried to track him down to interview him for myself, I was told the man had moved to California and checked into a rehab facility. I figured it was a dead end. He was either high or drunk the entire time we knew him. But now he's here and looks sharp as a tack. Maybe he remembers something."

"Do you think he's a suspect?" The hope in her voice darn near cracked his heart in two. He didn't want to lead her down a faulty path, but the investigator in him told him that he needed to talk to Rusty. "He was cleared by the police. But since I didn't interview him myself, I still have my doubts. There's only one way to find out. We investigate."

"It sounds like a lead to me." They took the next few flights in silence, and only their heavy breaths and footsteps echoed in the empty stairwell. As they reached the concrete steps on the main level, Jake slammed open the fire door. It reverberated with a loud thud, and they both spilled out onto a garden terrace section of the resort. A family of five was in the middle of taking a selfie by the waterfall, and they looked over with startled red faces at the commotion. These tourists clearly didn't take kindly to people bursting into their travel memory moment. "Excuse us, ma'am. Sir. Kids." That should cover the whole lot. "Sorry about the noise and the intrusion. We're in a...hurry."

He blew past them as Abby called out her own apology, and they broke into a run for the beach. Yet when they arrived, they were too late. The small group of surfers had made it out into the ocean. They'd have to wait till they came back in before he could question Rusty.

"Oh no, they're gone." She pulled her hand away as he realized he'd been holding it the entire time. It had warmed and comforted him. Brought him solace along with a shot of adrenaline that made him take the stairs at a pace he hadn't since the police academy.

He doubled over to catch his breath. Clearly, he needed to add stairs to his workout regime. "I should have known the drill. I wanted to catch him before he left, but there's still time. They'll be out in the water for half an hour. We can talk to him when he comes back."

She propped her hands on her hips. Her breathing was soft and recovered as if they hadn't just covered half a mile in five minutes. A frown graced her features, but it did nothing to diminish her beauty. Was it possible she felt the same pull he felt toward her? One he'd never noticed when they were growing up back in Michigan. No. he was imagining things. He chalked it up to the stress of dealing with this case once again.

"So what? We just wait?" She huffed out her sentence. And even that was cute.

He smiled over at her. "Yeah. Reporters are good at waiting, right? You put in what, two, three hours at the station this morning?"

She punched him on the arm. "You knew about that? Was it you that kept me waiting?"

He shook his head. "No. It was my partner. Benny. He's great, trust me. Even if he did make you wait."

He reached down and pulled off his heavy boots. Then came his socks, and he stuffed them into the boots and left them in a heap on the sand. Rolling up his khakis, he signaled to her. "C'mon. Let's wait in the waves."

He looked down, and she was barefoot. No shoes to abandon. She gave him a half shrug. "What can I say? I'm always prepared. Unlike you."

He smiled again and shook his head. Same old Abby. He'd definitely imagined the attraction. He took the lead as they walked across the sand that was still warm from the brilliant sunny day. When they reached the ocean, she stood beside him, and they watched the waves roll into the shore and then out again in a steady beat. The turquoise water was calm on the beach, but the waves just beyond the crest were good enough for surfing.

They stood close enough that the cool water lapped at their feet as it rose and fell. The soothing rhythm relaxed him for the first time today. The stress ebbed and flowed away from his body as he stood beside her. But it was surely the ocean that was having that effect on him. Wasn't it?

"This is nice. I can see why you love it here."

He let out a long slow breath. "I did love it. When Isaac was alive, this was our paradise. For two kids from the middle of Michigan to come here and experience all of this beauty as well as the surfing, it sure was something. But honestly, now? It's just my job. I have nowhere else to go."

He watched as she closed her eyes and drew in a breath. "I know what you mean. It's New York for me. That's where the news is. But at least I can enjoy this beach for a month while I'm here."

He nodded. "Yes, you can. Let's walk down to the pier to see the surfers better. I'll tell you if Rusty is doing a good job with his lessons or not."

She laughed. A light, airy sound he would never tire of hearing. "Great. I can't wait to hear how the great Jake Devereaux taught surfing."

He held up a finger. "Ah, it was Jacob back then. And don't worry. I'll tell you all about it."

She rolled her eyes, and he took that as a good sign. Even though they were solving a murder together, it didn't need to be doom and gloom all the time, although it seemed like that was what their lives had become. If he could make this just a little bit easier on her without losing his mind at the same time, he'd call this a win.

****

Half an hour later, the surfers piled back onto the beach. Smiles and bouts of laughter rose up in the group. Jake imagined they'd had a wonderful time out in the waves, and he hated to break up the merriment, but his patience wore thin after this long day.

He didn't waste any time marching over to them, badge in hand. Abby followed close behind him as he strode over to the older instructor who was bidding goodbye to his new protégés. He turned back to her. "You wait here, okay? I find it's easier on witnesses if they're not bombarded by more than one person. We don't want to spook him."

She shook her head. "No way. I'll let you take the lead, but this is the first solid clue we've had. I'm not missing out on this. Besides, you need me. I know this can't be easy for you to go through this all over again."

That was the understatement of the year. But what he needed to do was get his head on straight in order to question Rusty. Not think about grabbing her hand again. "Don't worry. I got this." Maybe if he said the words out loud, they'd suddenly become true.

She gave him a shrug. "I'll be right beside you, just in case."

He nodded his agreement. Besides, if they didn't hurry up, they'd lose Rusty, and then he'd have to try and track him down another way.

"Got a minute?" He called out, and the man turned away from the middle-aged woman who was beaming from ear to ear at him. Clearly, she'd just caught her first wave on her lesson.

He held up a finger to Jake and turned back to her. "Keep up the good work, Betty. Maybe I'll see you again before you head back to the mainland."

The woman gushed and headed back over to a group that looked like her family screaming the entire time about how awesome Hawaii was. Jake smiled.

He'd had more than a few clients like that way back when he'd taught surfing, and it was what had made the job so much fun. That and the waves, of course.

Rusty turned back to Jake and raked a hand through his short salt-and-pepper hair. Bright and alert green eyes stared back at him. Even with a dark tan, he looked ten years younger instead of ten years older. Jake was happy. It appeared as if the man had gotten his life back on track.

Rusty gave him a shrug. "Sorry, man. Lessons are done for the day. If you want, you can sign up at the shack for tomorrow."

"I don't want lessons." Jake held out his badge. "We just have a few questions for you."

The man studied his badge as he wiped salt water from his face. "State of Hawaii Investigator. That sounds official. Who's the little lady?"

Though Jake heard Abby groan under her breath, she offered a sweet smile at the older man. "I'm his consultant. But I don't have my badge with me. Will that be a problem?"

The man smiled back. "Not at all. How can I help you today?"

"I'm Lt. Jake Devereaux. This is Abigail. I don't know if you remember, but after I came to Hawaii ten years ago, you hired me and my friend, Isaac Hastings, as surfing instructors."

The man leaned in closer. His green gaze was sharper than Jake remembered all the years ago. "Jacob, is that you? Of course, I remember, man. And your buddy, Isaac. What a tragedy that was. Shook this whole place up for some time. I had to leave for a while. Get my life sorted out."

"I hear you, Rusty. I really do," Jake said.

"Look at you, a cop now?" His eyes went wide. "Hey, man, if you're here about all that stuff I used to do back in the day—"

Jake held up a hand. "I just needed to ask you a few questions. About Isaac's murder."

Rusty wrinkled his forehead. "What about it? I told those investigators back then everything I knew. I went to the disco with him. We partied it up to celebrate the upcoming weekend. Had some wings and a few beers, talked to a few ladies. Halfway through the night, he disappeared while I was dancing with a hula girl. When he didn't come back, I went searching for him. But he wasn't in the usual places, the bar, the washroom, or outside getting a breath of air. When I went around the back of the club to sneak back in, I found him in a heap out by the trash bin. Bloody and beaten to death. I called an ambulance, but it was too late."

The blasé manner his old boss used to describe the murder turned Jacob's stomach. He was used to gritty crime details. But not when they involved his best friend. He swallowed the bile rising in his throat. This was the reason he didn't want to get involved. Reliving the nightmare of losing Isaac might put him right back where he started.

"Yeah, I know. I read all that in the report." Had all the crime scene and autopsy pictures burned into his brain for eternity. "But I was just wondering. Did you see or hear anything else a couple of days or weeks before or after the murder that might explain who wanted Isaac dead?"

Rusty appeared thoughtful for a moment and then shook his head. "I don't think so. But I'm telling you, that murder woke me up. I got clean and sober after that at a clinic in California. But Hawaii was still in my blood. I came back here a year ago. To teach surfing again. I remember his murder like it was clear as day. But I don't know why anyone wanted to hurt Isaac. He was a good kid."

Jake nodded. "Yes. He was. So there's nothing you forgot to tell the police before you went to California? Nothing you remembered after you got clean?"

Rusty suddenly clapped his hands together. "Wait a minute. Yes. There was something. I called the police station from the clinic to tell them, but the call got dropped, and then I forgot again. Rehab isn't for the faint of heart, and it took all I had to focus on staying clean back then. I wanted to tell the investigators I saw someone arguing with Isaac a couple days before the murder."

As Jake's pulse picked up speed, he leaned closer to Rusty. "Who was it?"

He shrugged. "That I don't know. But it was someone I knew. I remember that much."

Jake put a hand on the man's shoulder. Something. Anything. To get him to remember. "Someone you knew. What does that mean? Was it someone from the resort? Your boss? Or one of our friends?"

He shook his head. "No. Not anyone like that. At least I don't think so." He tapped his head. "Geez. I wish I remember more. But that's all I've got. You know I wasn't too clearheaded back in the day. I know it was someone I'd seen around, but that's it. I'm sorry, buddy."

Jake let go of his shoulder and pulled a card out of his pocket. "If you remember anything, even if it seems insignificant, just give me a call, okay? And you're not planning on leaving town, are you?"

The man shook his head and studied the card. "No way. I'm here to stay this time. And I sure will give you a call if I remember anything. I wish I could help you and your girl solve the case."

Jake raised an eyebrow. "What?"

Rusty gave a toothy smile. "You two look good together."

"No. we're not a couple." The unison response from Abby and Jake echoed out onto the waves.

Jake cleared his throat. "We're working on the case together. That's all."

Rusty gave him a wink before he leaned down and picked up his surfboard. "Sure, sure. Anything you say. Hey, we should catch some waves sometime."

"Yeah, I'd like that." Rusty gave him the thumbs-up sign and sauntered away.

Abby came around to face him, her long hair fluttering in the light breeze and her cheeks pink. Was it possible Rusty's words affected her too? "So that was a dead end, huh? Unless you think he had something to do with the murder, and he doesn't remember."

Jake sighed and chalked up her pink cheeks to the warmth of the fading sun. She was all business, which was how it should be.

"I don't think so," he said. "The guy doesn't have a violent bone in his body, but I'm not ruling him out entirely as a suspect yet. It's sometimes common for the killer to pretend to have found the body when they've, in fact, done the killing. I have to check the notes I made. And he remembers something about Isaac arguing with someone, but it's not enough to go on. It is suspicious he left town just after the murder, even if his story does check out. I'm just not sure at this point. I guess we'll have to go back to the boxes and see what we can find."

She nodded. "Good idea. Let's burn the midnight oil and see what we can come up with."

He gave her a half shrug. They could burn whatever they wanted, and he'd done that too many times to count in this case, but he was reasonably sure they'd come up with nothing just like he had all those years ago.

****

They stopped for some shaved pineapple ice at a booth on the beach. The sweet fruity taste lingered in her mouth as they'd managed to hop on an empty cart. She squeezed his forearm. It was warm, comforting, and he didn't move away. He'd done a really good job interviewing Rusty, and she felt like she owed him for all of this. A lot more than sharing a dessert.

She laid a hand on Jacob's arm as the elevator ascended in a swift and speedy movement on the way back up to her hotel room. "When all this is over, we should do something fun. You work too hard."

He turned toward her. "Oh yeah? Like what do you consider fun these days?"

She laughed. "I don't know. Maybe a luau. You can't come to Hawaii and not do that, right?"

The elevator door flashed on seven and let out a ding signaling their floor. She pulled her hand away as they stepped off and immediately felt the absence of his strength, his support. Spooning another serving of dessert into her mouth, she moaned at the pure pleasure this simple treat offered her.

He gave her a half shrug. "Um, so I've heard."

Her mouth fell open, but she clamped it shut. Then it flew open again. "What? Don't tell me you've lived in Hawaii for a decade and have never been to a luau."

He chuckled. "Okay. I won't."

"I can't believe you. A luau is a must in Hawaii. That's it. We have to go. I'll book us in for one."

She pulled her cell phone out of her dress pocket to peruse the luau choices as they walked down the hall. About a foot from their door, she ran smack dab into Jacob's broad shoulders. She opened her mouth to protest, but her gaze traveled to where he pointed.

Her hotel room door was ajar.

She was sure she'd shut it behind her when they left. An alarm of adrenaline raced through her veins like chunks of ice flowing down a melting river. She dropped her dessert and let out a shiver as she put a hand to her wildly beating heart.

He pulled his handgun from its holster and motioned for her to go behind him. She didn't argue. He pulled the slide to load the chamber of the weapon. The bullet clicked into place with a soft smack as he pointed the firearm toward the open door and crept toward it.

Chapter Seven

Jake threw open the door, pointing the gun first in the direction of the open bathroom door and then around the room. Abby hovered as he cleared the balcony and the closets. No one was here, but someone had been. The room was a mess. Boxes were overturned, and her suitcase lay on its side with the contents spilling out onto the floor. The covers of the bed had been thrown to the side, and the leftovers from their earlier lunch had been tossed on the floor. They'd been looking for something, but what?

He re-holstered his weapon and ushered her into the room. Her legs wobbled as she moved back into the beautiful space that was now possibly tainted with more trouble. An invisible chill seemed to hover in the room, and she rubbed her bare arms to keep them from erupting in goose bumps.

He went to the balcony and leaned over, surveying left and right at the scene below, then he turned back to her. "No suspicious activity down on the beach. All looks calm. Whoever was here is probably long gone and went out of the front entrance. They must have left before we got back up here. Do you think you left the door open when we went downstairs?"

She shook her head. "I remember it shutting behind us because it closed with a loud thud. I didn't leave it open or unlocked, Jake."

He gave her a tight smile. It was probably meant to calm her, but it only managed to make her pulse tick faster. It was only hours ago someone had tried to kidnap her. And now this?

"They might have been watching the room. It may have just been some kids looking for cash. Let's see if anything's missing, and then I'll call it in."

She nodded and rummaged through the remains of her suitcase. She turned over the raspberry-colored case and piled her dresses and shorts back inside. All her clothes and the silver urns of her mother and brother's ashes remained intact along with a box of Isaac's things she'd brought with her. Her toiletries bag had been scattered, and some of her perfume had spilled onto the rug, but nothing was missing. Everything seemed in order. She'd placed her passport, extra cash, and the few pieces of jewelry she'd brought with her in the safe, and it remained untouched in the closet. "Well, if someone did break in, they didn't bother with the safe or take anything from my suitcase."

He nodded as he continued to comb the room for telltale signs of what the person was after. "The security here is good. I'll check the cameras later. If security saw anyone entering your room without reason, they would have notified us. But we'll check just the same."

"I have nothing. I don't know what they wanted." A bright white streak of panic rushed to Abby's chest, and she drew in a deep breath. "What about the files?"

His gaze darted around as if he could catalog everything in the blink of an eye. After what they'd talked about before, she wasn't ruling that out entirely. She surveyed the room. Many of the files lay scattered on the bed and the desk where they had been going over them. A few remained in a box on the balcony. But wait a minute. They'd left three boxes in here this afternoon. And now, only two remained. "One of the boxes is missing."

She ran over to see which one, but he shook his head. "Don't bother. I already know. The witness interview boxes are missing. The ones we wanted to go over after talking to Rusty."

She let out a long sigh and sat down on the bed. Putting her head in her hands, she took a deep breath. She wished she'd had more time to memorize the files, but she hadn't seen all of them before they ran down to the beach. "Do you think it was Rusty?"

He gave her a half shrug and settled beside her on the bed. He was close enough to touch, but she didn't dare. Even still, warmth radiated from his body, bringing comfort and easing the bitter coolness of the room. "Well, he has a good alibi. We were talking to him as this happened. But he could have gotten someone to do it for him. Yet I don't see how. He didn't even know about our visit. At least he seemed surprised."

She squeezed her hands into tight fists beside her in frustration. "Yes, he did. It was probably someone else. But we can't rule him out yet. Maybe it's someone who doesn't want us looking into the other possible witnesses since that was what was taken."

He nodded. "Possibly. From what I can remember, they interviewed a bunch of people that had come in contact with Isaac at the club that night. Rusty, the girls he spoke about meeting, the club manager, and the waitresses. Liko had also been there, but he left early and headed home. His mom and his sister vouched for him. And other than me, there weren't any other interviews that I can remember. I have some notes back at my place on the interviews. We can double-check those."

She put a hand to her chest. Her heartbeat had finally slowed back down to somewhere just above average. "What should we do now?"

He stood and shoved his fingers through his hair. Was he agitated about the case? Or was it something else? She couldn't tell for sure. He paced the length of the room, then grabbed a box and began stuffing papers inside. His flurry of movement made her head spin.

"Get your stuff together," he barked. "You're coming home with me."

His words barked an order, not a request. A big, growly police-issued order. She opened her mouth to protest, and he shot her a dark stare.

"You've had a threatening note left on your car, almost been kidnapped, and now your hotel room has been burgled. Even if you don't think you're in danger, trust me, you are. Someone doesn't want you looking into this case."

He had a point. Three, in fact. Her mouth turned dry, and fear clawed at her emotions, but she stamped it all down. Perhaps he was right. Maybe this wasn't just a cold case murder investigation anymore. But did she need his protection?

His brilliant blue gaze was laced with concern. "The only way I can continue to work on it with a clear mind is to make sure you're safe. And you will be at my house. I've got plenty of room at the cottage. Please don't argue with me. It's been a very long day."

She didn't want to argue. Not anymore. And she

wasn't prepared to leave Hawaii, so if she had to stay with him, she would. She just hoped the tingly feeling she got when he was close to her dissipated the more time they spent together. "Okay, thank you. I'll stay with you."

****

Jacob let out a long breath as he set the last of the boxes in his living room and padded into the kitchen. Abby was settling into the guest room, and he wanted to make something special for her for dinner. They'd been through a lot today, and maybe they deserved just a little bit of that break she was talking about.

He settled on making salad and pizza, not exactly a luau, but it would have to do. Besides, homemade Hawaiian pizza had always been her favorite. As he rolled the dough and chopped the pineapple, he made a mental note about all the things he needed to do with the case. This afternoon, he'd told the governor he needed some time off, although he didn't mention the exact reason why. She wholeheartedly agreed as he hadn't taken any leave for over a year since he'd gotten his life back. Work kept him centered. Focused.

After that, he arranged to have some DNA samples from the crime scene sent for retesting. Testing methods had come a long way in the last few years, and he needed to know if he could garner any leads on that front. It would also give him an idea if Rusty was involved. He had a criminal record, so he'd be on file if there was a hit. He also had notes here at home relating to the box that was stolen, so that was also something to go on.

As he put the pizza in the oven and poured two glasses of a sparkling pineapple juice from the island of

Maui, Abby appeared at the threshold of the kitchen.

"So you do cook. You held out on me the other day, didn't you?" A wide smile graced her beautiful features. She'd changed into maroon sweatshirt and black tights. Her outfit reminded him of their young, carefree days. He'd swapped his dress shirt and khakis for a black T-shirt and shorts, so now it was as if they were just a couple of teenagers again.

He gave a half shrug. "Maybe a little. It's not quite a luau. But it is Hawaiian."

Her eyes went wide, and a smile graced her lips. "Hawaiian pizza? A man after my own heart."

She clutched her chest as she laughed and moved into the kitchen. Was he a man after her heart? He already liked having her here, and she'd barely been here an hour. He never cooked when he was on his own, and the first thing he did after he showed her his room was go to the kitchen and rummage around in the fridge. He saw himself getting used to this.

But he couldn't. Shouldn't. If his ex had taught him anything, it was he wasn't cut out for relationships. Besides, in the ten years they'd been apart, he'd done the one thing she would never understand. Or forgive him for.

"What can I do to help?" She came up beside him as he tossed veggies into a salad bowl.

He handed her a glass of pineapple juice, and the glass tinkled with the ice cubes he'd added. "Nothing. Everything is taken care of. I've got some notes here, and we can still burn the midnight oil. It just might be a bit delayed."

A small smile tugged at the corner of her lips. "You really want to burn the midnight oil, don't you?"

He smiled back. "What I want is to solve this case and get you back to the mainland. I didn't protect your brother, but I'm going to protect you."

She reached for his hand, and he let her take it. Her soft skin seemed to melt his frozen heart ever so slightly. But these feelings weren't real. It couldn't last. Nevertheless, he held on to her hand like a drowning sailor clinging to a life raft.

"What happened to Isaac isn't your fault." Her voice was low, a tranquil melody that spoke to his soul.

He squeezed her hand and then pulled away. She wouldn't say that if she knew what he'd done. He didn't deserve her kindness. Turning away, he ran a rough hand through his scalp. "Yes, it is. I should have been there for your brother the night he was murdered, and I wasn't. I'll never forgive myself."

She pursed her lips. "I don't blame you. Neither would Isaac if he could tell you that himself."

Was it true what she was saying? Maybe for her and for the clean-cut kid he used to be, but now for him, he was sure could never get over this. She was wrong.

She sighed and gave herself a hug he should be offering. Her words had somehow cooled and deflated the tension he'd been holding on to for so long. The timer on the stove buzzed, signaling dinner was ready, and he was relieved for the reprieve. He didn't like talking about his feelings anymore, although it seemed natural with her. But no, he wasn't going down that path again. "Pizza's ready. I hope you're hungry."

She smiled. "I'm always hungry. I still have that bottomless pit of a stomach."

He smiled back. "Good."

He handed her a plate he'd set on the table, and she filled half of it with salad and the other with piping-hot pineapple and ham pizza. He did the same.

He gestured through the kitchen. "We can eat out on the porch. It's a mild night."

She nodded, and they walked through the house and out onto the lanai where they'd sat on the day she'd arrived. Leo was lounging on one of the chairs, and he perked up his head at the smell of fresh-baked pizza.

She smiled. "Does he eat pizza?"

Jacob laughed. "No. I just let him have some of the ham. And just for the record, I also feed him cat food. Lots of it."

Abby smiled. "Okay," she said as she peeled off a piece of meat and leaned over to feed it to the cat. He purred and licked his lips. Then he got up, did a cat stretch, and sauntered off in search of more dinner. "He's so cute. Maybe I should get a pet."

He nodded. "Maybe you should. I like having him around. Even if he does eat all my food." Setting the plates down on the table in front of them, she chose a single chair, and he opted for the love seat. As he collapsed into the comfort of the cushions, he felt the stress of the day catching up with him.

The night was upon them, and the inky sky was awash with a million bright yellow bursts of stars. He often sat out here after work, listening to the gentle lull of the waves and staring at the wonder of this land as he pondered how his life got so off track. But it was on track for now. As long as he didn't let this case or his feelings for Abby overtake him.

"It's beautiful out here," she said, breaking the silence of the night.

He tilted his head to the sky and breathed in a breath of fresh, cool salty air. "Yes. I love the beach. Day or night."

She toyed with a lock of her hair that fell in waves down her shoulders. "Me, too."

They picked up their plates and ate in silence for a beat. Having her here made everything brighter, more alive. Even the still of the night. He always thought he'd have this. A relationship. Someone to love. But it was never in the cards for him. And that's the way it would always be.

She gazed over at him in the semidarkness. The string lights of the porch cast an angelic glow on her features, and if he thought the night sky was gorgeous, she was a million times more so.

"What happened, Jake? I mean, what really happened after Isaac died? It seems like you became a whole different person."

He paused before answering. How much did he want to tell her? He'd start at the beginning and see how far he got. Yet if he got to the end of his sordid tale, she'd no longer be smiling at him like she was right now. And he liked her smile.

"In a way, I did. At first, I was so focused on the police academy and getting a job with the Honolulu Police Department. After that, I had the skills, and I desperately wanted to solve Isaac's murder. I thought I would feel less guilty if I somehow knew who murdered him and that they were brought to justice. Instead, it turned into a nightmare."

Her eyes became sad, and he wanted to bite back the words he'd just spoken. But she deserved the truth—at least part of it.

"How so?"

He took a bite of pizza before answering. As if the warm cheesy mix could settle his tumultuous past. "I wanted a normal life. I had a good job and a roof over my head, not anything like how we grew up. The past was nothing but misery with my mom dying in childbirth and being raised by a drug-addicted father. I thought as a police officer, I was past all that. Matured and moved on if you will."

She set down her glass after taking a sip. "You were always mature. Not anything like your father."

He was almost exactly like his father, but he wasn't going there. Not tonight. "You always see the best in everybody. That's what I always loved about you."

"Touché," she said, throwing her earlier words back at him.

He laughed and speared a forkful of lettuce. Even the silence between them was natural. Comfortable. "Anyways, for a while, it worked. I met a girl, dated, and even got engaged, but your brother's death still haunted me. I became obsessed with the case. Nothing else mattered. Not even my relationship. I might not have been addicted to drugs like my father, but I was still consumed. For me, it was all about who murdered my best friend."

"I'm sorry. I had no idea the case affected you this way." She put down her plate and reached over and grabbed his hand in hers. This time, enveloped in her warmth, he didn't pull away.

He rubbed his bearded chin. "There was no way for you to know. We stopped talking while I was still at the academy. But I was always planning on solving the case and telling you who needed to be brought to justice. Except I never could. None of my leads panned out, my fiancée left me, and I almost lost my job. Isaac was my best friend, and I know he'd do the same for me if the roles were reversed. And I can't tell you how many nights I wished that. I still do."

She pulled away and put a hand to her throat. As if what he'd said had injured her. "No. You can't think like that. You and I are still here for a reason. A purpose."

He squeezed her hand. "Maybe. But I just don't think our purpose is to solve this murder. Not after I tried for so many years and failed. That's why I didn't want you to look into this case. Like I told you before, I've been over it a million times. I'm not sure we're going to find anything new."

She folded her hands in her lap, and he could see hope blooming in her eyes. "But we already have. We found Rusty. He might be our suspect."

"And possibly the one who's been putting you in danger."

****

Abby's blood ran cold at the mention of her in danger again. She'd shrugged off the note and the almost kidnapping, but now someone was interfering with the investigation outright. Was it possible Jacob was right about how much danger she was in? She had to put it out of her mind, or she'd never solve the case. She gave him what she hoped was a bored shrug. "Do you really think he's capable of that? He seemed like just a regular surfer dude to me." That much was true, but she knew from experience appearances could sometimes be deceiving.

"I'm not sure. But we are going to get to the

bottom of this. The note is a dead end since you threw it away, but we've got a BOLO out for the car, and the HPD is going over your hotel room to search for forensic evidence the intruder might have left behind. We'll find out who's after you and if it has anything to do with the murder. Which it's looking more and more like it might be connected. But don't worry, I'll keep you safe."

The words he spoke radiated in her chest. She did feel safe with him. But she couldn't explain why. Why did her heart skip a beat every time they got close to each other? Sure, she'd had a harmless crush on him all those years ago, but now they'd grown up. Neither were cut out for relationships, not to mention they lived five thousand miles apart. Yet even still.

He pulled his hand away and stood to gather the dishes. "Listen, you must be exhausted. Why don't we start over with the case fresh in the morning? You go on and get some rest, and I'll clean up."

She raised an eyebrow at him. She'd seen the way he cleaned up. And in the past, he'd rather take a wrecking ball to the kitchen than wash dishes properly. "I'll help you with the dishes."

He shook his head. "No, I insist, I got it."

She scoffed. "Oh, like the time you were in charge of cleaning up your place after having a few friends over turned into a few hundred. You threw perfectly good dishes in the trash and swept the rest of the mess under the rug."

He smiled at the memory but waved her off. "That was then. I've gotten older and wiser since then. I don't throw out dishes anymore. It's too expensive to replace them."

"Just the same, I'll help. You wash, and I'll dry, then we both need a good night's sleep so we can get back to the case tomorrow."

He picked up their dishes. "Okay."

They trudged into the kitchen, dirty dishes in hand, and she watched as he filled the sink. When it was filled with warm frothy water, he dumped the dishes in. But instead of washing them, he blew a wad of bubbles in the air.

"You still do that?" she asked as she felt them settle in her hair. He might be older, but apparently, he hadn't outgrown this teenage trait.

"Yup. And I'm sorry, but you got some—" He reached over with a soapy hand and piled more bubbles on her hair.

"Oh yeah?" She retorted and scooped up a handful herself, planting the entire blob smack dab in the middle of his smirking face. Then it was on.

Bubbles flew back and forth until there was none left in the sink, and the dishes still weren't washed. Leo, who had been watching them from the sidelines, took off as soon as the soap started to fly. He reached into a bottom drawer and pulled out some towels. Dropping a few on the wet granite tile, he handed one to her. She dried her face and tried to stop laughing. He was suddenly the same old boy she'd always known.

He took a towel and dried his face, then he gazed at her. "You still got some, here." He reached over with a tender hand and wiped her hair by her ear. Electricity hummed in the air as his fingers grazed her cheek, and then he cupped her chin in his palm and brought her closer.

She raised her cloth. "You've still got some here."

She wiped above his eyebrow as his gaze penetrated her very core. She closed her eyes as he leaned into her and murmured something about playing with fire.

His lips were on hers, firm and warm. And all thoughts of anything except them, together, scattered like the seeds of a flower in the light wind. She wound her arms around his neck and inhaled his sea salt and bergamot scent as he pulled her closer. The shrill sound of his phone rang out, piercing the quiet of the moment. Her eyes flew open, and he pulled away. The spell was broken.

He turned away from her and reached into his back pocket to retrieve the ringing device. "Devereaux," he said as cool as a cucumber. As if they hadn't just shared a moment seconds ago. But maybe it was for the best. What had she been thinking kissing him? And he kissing her? It could never work.

After a few more beats and some grunting, he disconnected the call and turned to her. "About that. I'm sorry. I was way out of line. That never should have happened. And it won't again. I promise you."

She nodded. Good. They were on the same page. She felt her cheeks flush warm. "Oh yeah. Of course. I get it. We just got caught up in the moment. But we need to focus on the case."

He murmured something she didn't quite catch. "Yes, that's right. And speaking of which, they found the car that tried to abduct you, but the perp was long gone. Forensics is going over it to see if there are any prints. Although it's doubtful as he was wearing gloves. But just in case, they're going to go over it with a fine-tooth comb. And they are running the partial plate to see which cars on the island match the description of the sedan."

She nodded. "Good, that's good. Should we go to the station and get an update?"

He shook his head. "Nah. The team will let me know. We can talk to them in the morning. Now, you should go, get some sleep."

She nodded and turned away from him. She didn't know how much she'd sleep with the memory of his arms around her, and his lips on hers, searing her memory banks. But she'd have to. It was nothing—a one-off mistake. So how come it felt so right?

Chapter Eight

Jake tossed and turned in his king-sized bed, but it didn't bring him the rest he so greatly needed. No. It only managed to wrap his bedsheets in a messy heap at his feet. He'd read that chilled, dark rooms with cool color schemes lowered blood pressure to help ensure a decent night's sleep. And although he didn't mind the indigo shades the owner had chosen for the furnishings that worked well with the original wood paneling, they were anything but soothing tonight.

He was hotter than the Mauna Loa volcano when it was erupting on the big island and wide awake. Although it wasn't a shot in the dark to conclude the cause was his house guest sleeping only a few feet away that was causing his sleepless night. Not his lack of relaxing surroundings. He couldn't get her sweet coconut-scented skin out of his mind.

He wanted to blame it on the case. The stress they'd both been through the day before and the open and honest conversation they'd shared last night over luau pizza. He hadn't revealed everything, but he'd said enough. Even still. What had he been thinking? He hadn't. And he vowed that would never happen again. But what to do now?

Letting out a low groan, he sat up. There was no sense prolonging this futile effort to get some shut-eye. Besides, it was approaching dawn and time to get up to face the day. A day that was jam-packed with going over the rest of the files and seeing what his team had come up with overnight.

He had to concentrate. And not on Abby. She was a temptation he couldn't afford. Didn't deserve after the implosion of his last relationship. If he let her down like he had Tamara, he'd never forgive himself. Also, she didn't know Jake. The real Jake. She deserved better.

Shaking his head to clear his erratic thoughts, he got up and threw on some black lounging pants and a gray T-shirt, then padded down the hallway toward the kitchen.

This cottage on the beach should have brought him comfort. It was everything he ever wanted in a house, even if he didn't own it. It was a completely renovated modern affair that preserved most of the original features of the home that was built in the fifties, except the owner had added every modern amenity. But in the end, it was only just a house. And he wanted so much more. Yet he could never allow himself anything but his work. Everything else just cost too much.

After putting on the latte machine in the kitchen and taking care to make enough for him and Abby, he poured a cup. Then he fed an eagerly awaiting Leo his breakfast and refreshed his water. Once Leo was chowing down, he took his latte outside to the garden patio. The fresh air was cool, but he welcomed the chill after his fitful and overheated slumber. He dropped into a padded chair and stared up at the sky.

The dark night receded, leaving in its wake a burst of yellow-orange that streaked across the sky. He watched as the clouds parted, giving way to a baby-blue hue that would brighten as the day went on. The sun tilted, then glinted off the edge of the ocean in the distance, giving it an ethereal glow. This sight never failed to lift his spirits and remind him that he was in the right place.

He took a deep breath of the brisk morning air and sighed. Being off-balance for the last couple of days had wreaked havoc on his schedule, but if he was being honest with himself, it had also awakened in him long-dormant thoughts. Thoughts of what if. Thoughts he had no business thinking.

"Wow," came a soft voice from behind him, and he sat up and turned toward her. It was as if when he thought of her, she appeared. But he was too much of a realist to believe in fanciful concepts like karma and destiny that Grace was always going on about.

"This view is…magnificent." He watched as her gaze traveled across the patio to the scene in the distance. The courtyard was filling with light, and streaks of sunlight bounced off the windows of the house. The clouds had cleared, and the sky was a bright cerulean backdrop to the perfectly manicured lawn and ocean in the distance. He murmured his agreement and stood up. The view was striking. But he wasn't talking about the grass.

She tore her gaze away from the sunrise and smiled over at him. And that gesture alone was more stunning than the hundreds of times he'd watched the sky change over the backdrop of this paradise. She was dressed in pale-pink striped flannel pajamas, clutching a steaming latte in her hands, and her ebony hair was in loose waves raining down her shoulders.

"Sorry to disturb you," she said and turned to go back inside. "I didn't think you were out here, and I saw the sun rising from the kitchen. I just had to come out and see it for myself."

"No bother," he managed to say and gestured to the seat beside him, then sat down himself. "Please, come and join me."

She nodded and padded over to him in fluffy white socks but stopped just short of the chair. "Really, it's okay. I can see you were having some quiet time to yourself. I'll just go and get ready, then we can go over your files."

"I insist. This is the best spot in the entire house to have coffee. You have to sit and have a least one cup. Then we can get to work."

She pursed her lips but then nodded and sat down. That was if perching on the edge of the chair like a small bird about to take flight was considered sitting. Why was she so nervous? She tilted her face toward the ocean, and he noticed a flush crawl up her face. Ah yes. The elephant in the room. Last night. Should he mention it? The fact that he had no business doing what he did wasn't lost on him either. It had been a mistake. He was lost. In more ways than one. Time to make amends. "Again, about last night. I was out of line. I'm sorry."

Her wide dark gaze shot back to his, and coffee sloshed over the top of her cup as she jammed it down on the table in front of her. "No. No need to be sorry. In fact, let's just forget about the whole thing. Chalk it up to a late night and too much time poring over files, okay?"

"Sure. That sounds like a plan." It was a plan, all right. And one he had to stick to. For both of their sakes.

****

"What? Are you sure?"

Abby heard the agitation in Jacob's voice as he drilled down the evidence his team had gathered last night.

"Yes, I'm sure," said Kai. He was a Hawaiian and reminded her a little bit of Isaac with his dark handsome looks. Although his uniform of the day screamed police personnel. All of the team, including Kai, Benny, and Grace, were dressed in black polo shirts with the HPD logo on it and khaki pants. Jacob had on another black T-shirt with jeans this morning.

Abby felt way underdressed and out of place in her navy crop pants and white peasant blouse. At least she was able to remove the bandages from her hands this morning, making her feel less like a victim. A few red scrapes remained, but they would be gone in a few days. She was a part of this now and wanted to hear every word the team said. Even if she felt a little like she was a child eavesdropping on a grown-up conversation.

"It looks like this wasn't some random kidnapping or hotel burglary," Kai continued. "Although we were quite sure the break-in at the hotel at least had something to do with the case given the stolen files. Good thing for us, the perps got lazy. Left a print on the gas nozzle in the car and one on the door handle at the hotel. It's the same person. The bad news is that he's not in the database."

"Recheck it."

Jake paced the length of the living room as she, Kai, Benny, and Grace sat around his white wood dining table with its intricate gray-and-white marbled top. She was sure police business wasn't generally conducted in such luxury, but Jacob insisted the team come to his place to update him as he didn't want Abby out and about until the person who tried to kidnap her was caught. And this was a fact she agreed with. For the time being, at least.

"Okay, lieutenant. Whatever you say."

With a nod, Kai wrote something in his leather memo book. Grace and Benny sipped on lattes and picked at sweet Hawaiian bread. Everyone looked exhausted, and she felt a stab of guilt to the chest. The reason they'd been up all night was because of her.

Jake stopped and held up a hand. "On second thought, don't. I'll do it today. You guys worked all night on this, and you still have other police work to do. Abby and I will take over. You guys go get some shut-eye before you have to report to the governor."

Grace shook her head. She didn't have the carefree air of yesterday with her sidearm strapped to her side, and her hair pulled back into a severe bun. But she'd smiled at Abby the same way she had yesterday. Abby had warmed toward her instantly, even though they barely knew each other.

"No way," Grace said. "We're all in on this. We want to help you. You'd do the same for us."

Benny and Kai murmured their agreement, and Abby was touched by how close-knit and genuine this group was. Sure, she had a few friends and lots of colleagues at work, but this team was more like a family. Brothers and sisters who would do anything for each other.

It was something she always thought she'd do without after she'd come to grips with Isaac's death.

Yet every once and a while, she'd notice a family or two touring the streets of New York, and her heart ached, just a little. Jacob was lucky to have found a new family. And she'd just have to accept that wasn't in the plan for her.

Jacob cleared his throat. "Thanks, guys. I appreciate the offer. Abby and I will sort through the files today while you guys catch up, then maybe we can talk later and go over what we've discovered."

Jacob sounded calm, confident, and in charge. It seemed like he no longer doubted they'd solve the case. And with this team of experts, how could they not? Relief bubbled up inside her. They'd catch her brother's killer. It was only a matter of time. This was what she was here for. Nothing else.

"Sounds good," piped up Benny, and then he yawned. He rubbed his face as if it would help to wake him up, and his dark bloodshot eyes looked tired, probably because he hadn't closed them in way too long.

"Go on, get some rest." Jacob gestured to the threesome at the table. "We've got work to do."

As Jacob saw the group to the door, Abby wandered over to a box of Isaac's belongings on the coffee table. She'd brought it with her in her suitcase just in case it might help. It was sent to her about nine years ago after the police deemed his case cold, but she hadn't been able to bring herself to open it. Now, she had to. As she sat and touched the lid, her cell phone rang. She pulled it out of her pants pocket and peered at the display. *Unknown Caller* flashed back at her.

Since she was used to people blocking their number, especially when she received confidential evidence, she picked up on the second ring. She'd sent some off-the-record requests to a few confidential contacts last night and was hopeful it was one of them getting back to her. "Abigail Hastings."

"Don't open that box in your hand. Or any other evidence you have. We are watching you." A rough, computer disguised voice came over the line. Even if she did know the person, there was no way she'd be able to make out who it was with the heavy artificial effects.

A chill ran up her spine. First, they wrote a note, then tried to kidnap her. Now when she was in a place where she finally felt safe, she was in jeopardy again. Her pulse quickened, and she gripped the phone with her damp palms, steeling herself to be strong and think like a journalist, not a victim. "Who is this? Tell me now. If you stop this, you'll have a better chance of not going to prison for an awfully long time. Fess up."

"Never mind. You'll never figure out who we are. This is your last warning. If you don't stop looking into your brother's case, we'll kill you too."

After the line went dead, her phone fell from her grasp and crashed to the floor.

****

As Jake waved goodbye to his team, he heard Abby scream for the second time in two days. He slammed the door shut and ran back into the living room. She was standing in the middle of the floor, staring open-mouthed at her cell phone, which lay smashed on the granite tile. Her arms were spread eagle, and her fingers clenched as if she were holding on to an invisible object.

He ran to her and laid a hand on her shoulder. "Are

you okay? What happened?"

She looked up with fury in her dark eyes. "Someone just called. Told me to stop looking into the case. I was about to open a box; they said don't do it. My phone slipped out of my hand when the line went dead. Oh, no!"

She crouched down on the floor and started gathering up broken pieces of glass and plastic. "Ouch!" She clutched her thumb as it turned bright red.

He grabbed a napkin from the nearby table and pressed it to her hand. "Hey, take it easy. I'll get a broom and sweep this up. The glass is sharp. I don't want you hurting yourself again."

He realized he was holding her hand again; this time it was strictly professional. Nevertheless, every time he touched her, a bit of his soul gravitated toward hers. He pushed those thoughts out of his head as she stood and pulled her hand away.

"It's fine. Just a scratch, I think."

"Good. Don't worry about the phone. We need this one as evidence now. I'll get you a new one with additional security features so this won't happen again." He pulled his own phone out of his pants pocket and dialed. "Hey, sorry, guys. I need one more favor. Can you head back and take Abby's phone in as evidence? The killer just called her, and although it's not likely, we might be able to trace the call. Also, can you check the shoreline? She said someone was watching her, and I don't want to leave her alone."

After another short exchange, Jake thanked them and hung up. "Are you okay? I need to check something out. I'm not going far."

She gave the mess on the floor a forlorn look.

"Yeah, I'm fine. It's just my whole life is on that phone. I can't believe I dropped it. They said they would kill me. Just like they did my brother."

He wasn't too surprised. This case was escalating fast, and since Abby wasn't backing off, the killer was getting even more hostile. "I'm not going to let anything happen to you." Could he make that promise? He just did. And now he made another one. "And I'll see if the techs can get your information off your phone for you to put into your new one. Hang tight. I'll be right back."

"I'll write down everything the caller said. Maybe there's a tiny clue in there. I'll give it to your team when they get here."

"Good thinking."

She grabbed pen and paper from the table and took a seat on the couch as he ran through to the kitchen and let himself out into the backyard. With the property secured by fences and monitored by cameras, there was no way someone could come onto his land. He'd check once more of course, but he couldn't lose the feeling the killer was watching them another way.

It was another sunny day in Honolulu, so he wasn't surprised to see a lot of boats just offshore. Which one was watching them? He'd promised to keep her safe and almost failed again. Although Abby seemed more concerned about her phone than the threat.

The opposite was true for him. The killer was getting closer. Bolder. Aggressive. He wasn't sure how much time they had to try and solve the case before they'd try another kidnapping. Or worse. After taking a call from the team telling him they had another emergency, so he'd have to bring the cell phone to the techs himself, he called the local coastguard unit and asked them to be on the lookout for suspicious vessels near his property. Then he headed back to the house. "You sure you're okay?"

She sat on the sofa, staring at a small gray box on the table he'd never seen before. As she wound a gauze bandage around her thumb, she glanced up and gave him a watery smile. "I knew solving Isaac's case would be hard, yet this is harder than I imagined."

That made two of them. He took a seat next to her but didn't take her hand. Now that he knew where that sort of thing led, he wasn't about to do anything like that again. "I know what you mean. I'm sorry. But if the killer is now contacting you personally, maybe we're getting close. Did the threat scare you?"

She shook her head and gave him a narrow-eyed look that could easily make any seasoned criminal cower. "No. I'm just worried we're not going to be able to solve the case with all of these roadblocks being thrown up in our faces. Every time something like this happens, it stalls us. Takes us away from the case."

"Or closer. The threats and the murder have to be related. I'm sure of that now. If we solve one case, we solve another. Now we have more chances to catch who killed Isaac and who is threatening you."

She nodded. "Yes, I guess you're right."

He pointed to the table, and she continued to stare at it, not meeting his gaze. "What's that box?"

After a long pause, she glanced at him. "It contains Isaac's things. I brought them with me from the mainland. The police mailed it to me after they closed the case. I thought there might be a clue in there but now I'm not so sure. It's probably just old banking papers or something."

"There's only one way to find out. Unless you'd rather not?"

When she paused, he stood to give her some space. He wouldn't force her to open it. Besides, the police had probably vetted it before they gave it to her. He was sure it held his friend's belongings, but nothing of significance.

"I want to. But can you sit with me? Can we do it together?"

****

Abigail heard the pleading in her voice and hated it. She and Jacob had to work together and share the same roof, but he was also becoming a good friend again. One who offered his help when she couldn't face this task alone. If she'd been able to, she would have opened the box nine years ago, but she hadn't, and she needed his support.

Jacob nodded and sat back down next to her. "Of course. I'm here for you."

"Okay. You go." She gestured for him to lift the lid. He did and then took her hand in his as the smiling face of her and Isaac in an old childhood photo lay on top of a stack of papers.

She squeezed his hand for support. "Oh my," she said as she picked up the photo. "This is an old picture. We were maybe eight and four."

He nodded. "Yup. He always carried that photo in his wallet. I asked him one day why he didn't have a more recent picture. He said that it was because it's the last one he could remember where you were both so innocent. After you and he got older, you realized other parents didn't act the way yours did. That normal, happy families existed who didn't have a mother who drank too much and a father who left them. He loved that picture. And he loved you."

Fat tears rolled down her cheeks. He released her hand and leaned over and swiped them away with a gentle hand as she picked up the photo and studied it. Yes, it was exactly as he'd said. The picture had been taken outside a dilapidated white clapboard house they lived in on the edge of town. The place wasn't much, but it was theirs—until their mother could no longer afford to pay the bills and they'd been forced to move into a rent-controlled apartment in town.

"Why didn't I remember he had this photo?"

"You were so little. And he probably didn't want to bring up bad memories. But you guys were super cute. And innocent."

Her heart sank. What other things had Isaac kept from her? He'd protected her, she'd always known that, but not until she saw the photo did she understand how early his care started. He was a child trying to protect another child. And then he died so young.

Abby straightened her spine. She needed to avenge his murder. She needed to focus on the case. Her wants and needs no longer mattered.

She grabbed a tissue from the box on the table and wiped her own eyes. Then she stood up to pace the length of the living room. Maybe bringing this box hadn't been a good idea. It was just full of memories, and there probably wasn't anything in it. Besides, it would only slow them down if every five minutes she took a trip down memory lane. "Maybe going through this box is a waste of time. It's probably just more pictures showing how we grew up so poor. I don't need to see them."

"Do you want me to go through it?" Jacob asked. "See if there's anything, just in case."

This was silly. Why was she letting an old dusty box of papers make her so emotional? If there was something, anything in this box to help the case, she'd regret it forever if she didn't see everything for herself. "Let's do it together. It will make the task faster."

"Okay."

She took a seat beside him as he leafed through a pile of unpaid bills.

"Do you think any of these debts might be cause for murder?" There was more than she expected, and she'd learned in her time as a journalist that people were killed for much less than that.

His forehead crinkled in concentration. "I don't think so. They're all from legitimate companies. But I won't rule it out entirely."

Another dead end. She leaned over to shuffle through the box. There was a bunch of surfing medals, forms and certificates from various contests Isaac had participated in. One receipt was attached to a form, so worn and old she had to peel it off. She was about to put this down when something caught her eye—the date. "Look at this. This is a surfing competition Isaac registered for. It occurred a few days after he died."

He frowned. "I don't remember him getting ready for a competition before he was murdered." He took the piece of paper out of her hand and studied it. "I think I would have remembered this one. It was a biggie." He pointed to the logo for World's Pro Surfing printed at the top of the page.

She shrugged. This wasn't getting them anywhere.

"Maybe you just forgot? Like I forgot about that photo? A lot happened around the murder. I'm sure surfing was the furthest thing from your mind."

"Yeah, you're probably right. I'm sorry. I must have forgotten about it with everything else that went on that week. I don't think there's anything here that can help us."

His cell phone rang. He pulled it out of his pocket and glanced at the display before answering. She held her breath in anticipation of news on the case. A clue, even a small one, would be able to spur her on.

"Devereaux," he said into the phone.

A faint voice was heard on the other end of the line, but she couldn't make out what they were saying.

"Uh-huh," he said. "Are you sure?"

More mumbling on the other end of the line.

"Oahu Correctional? The last six months? Okay. Thanks, buddy. I owe you one."

He disconnected and turned. "That was Benny. He's still working our case while working another one. I'm telling you that guy doesn't sleep."

"What did he say?"

"I put a rush on the DNA recheck. The forensics people have matched some unidentified blood samples found at the scene of the murder. Looks like we may have found your brother's killer."

Chapter Nine

Jake drove his brand-new SUV with breakneck speed to the Oahu Correctional Facility on the other side of the island where the suspect was currently being incarcerated. As he traveled along the asphalt-paved interstate highway, he pressed on the gas. Native trees and grasses growing on the edge of the road blew past them like a blur. The road was busy with cars and trucks. He weaved in and out of traffic, the occasional horn blasting around them as he explained to Abby what Benny had told him.

"This guy, Freddy Preston, is a petty thug. He flew under the radar for most of his life, thanks to his hotshot lawyer father. Six months ago, even dear old Dad couldn't get the judge to drop the drug case against his son. Freddy got a fiver. As is now regulation, a sample of his DNA was taken and submitted into the database. It turns out it's a match to the blood that was found on Isaac at the scene of the crime."

She tightened her seatbelt and leaned over toward him. "Do you know him?"

"Yes. And no. We ran in the same circles because Freddy was also a surfer. He was friends with Liko. I'll give him a call later to see if he remembers anything. But we didn't hang out with Freddy, and I don't know why Isaac had anything to do with him. I guess we'll just have to hear his story."

She nodded. "Yes, we will. Thank you."

"Don't thank me yet. But I must admit, this is the first solid lead we've had." He stole a glance at her wide eyes. Full of expectation. He didn't want to give her false promise, but he was beginning to feel something he hadn't known he still possessed. Hope.

She pulled down the sun visor to shade her eyes and turned back to him. "Do you think Rusty Collins and Freddy have any connection?"

He didn't want to give her the wrong information since he wasn't sure himself, but he couldn't deny the possibility. "Yeah. Maybe. They knew each other. Of course, Freddy wasn't the one who ransacked the hotel room. He's been in prison for the last six months. But I've seen it where guys on the inside will get guys on the outside to do them favors. We'll keep it in mind. And the first question I'm going to ask him is about Rusty."

Jake took a sharp left and got off the highway. As he turned left and roared down a side street, he pulled up to the guard tower that was the first building in what he was sure was the ugliest place on the island. Over the years, he'd come here to solve a lot of crimes. Barbed wire atop a thick chain-link fence surrounded the four-story concrete building with its dark-red roof. OCF housed most of the criminals on the island. And it wasn't built to be pretty; it was built to be inescapable.

He slowed down his vehicle at the booth and flashed his badge to a keen-eyed young guard in a dark-blue uniform. His innocent smile said he was probably fresh out of college and resigned to traffic duty until he got his feet wet, hoping to hell he could handle what was inside when the time came.

The officer told him to proceed to the maximum-security section. Jake thanked him, and he pulled through the gate. After taking a short road, he pulled into a big lot that was filled with cars of every shape and size. He wasn't used to it being this busy. It took a few moments, but he finally found a parking spot in the last row. As he cut the engine, he turned toward her.

"Maybe you should wait here." He wasn't patronizing her. He just didn't want her exposed to whatever they were going to face inside. Even he wasn't sure he'd keep his cool if, in fact, Freddy had killed Isaac. He didn't want her to have to experience any more hardship. She deserved the peace she was seeking, and this was not it.

She huffed and crossed her arms across her chest. "Do you know how many prison interviews I've done? I've lost count, but it's a lot."

He sighed and yearned to reach out to her. "I know you've never done one on a suspect that possibly killed your brother. Let me handle this. Let me protect you. Just this once."

She shook her head. "I'm going in. I'll wait in the reception area. But the only reason I'm doing that is because I don't want the suspect getting away on a technicality because a civilian reporter was present during a police interview. I've seen enough people get off on less than that, and it's not right. If he is the killer, the victim's sister shouldn't be there when you make the arrest. I'll rely on you to ask the tough questions."

With a nod, he pulled on dark shades. "I will. I promise."

****

Abby trudged behind Jake as they approached the

main glass doors of the prison. She shielded her eyes from the bright sun. Her sunglasses lay somewhere at the bottom of her purse, and she didn't feel like fishing them out. As she stared up at the big yellow *Oahu Correctional Facility* sign, her heart sank. This concrete jungle, like many others she'd seen in her time as a reporter, was a sign of the times. Even in the middle of paradise, something like this had to exist. It was heartbreaking.

As they approached the building, he held the glass door open for her. Another glass door, this one locked and meshed with wire, greeted them as they stepped inside. Jacob flashed his badge at the camera, and a loud buzzing sound signaled their admission. He held the heavy door open for her, and she stepped inside. Much like the police station, this prison didn't look like they were in Hawaii anymore. Whitewashed walls and a drab gray linoleum floor with uncomfortable bare metal chairs bolted to the ground made up the waiting room. This place actually made the police station seem homey. She shivered despite the fact it wasn't cold in here. "I'll wait over there." She gestured to the row of chairs.

"I'll be out as soon as I know something."

She took a cursory glance around. It wasn't like she could get lost. The waiting room was only just bigger than a broom closet. She guessed they didn't entertain a lot of visitors here; they must be in another area. She tried on a smile but was afraid it came out more as a grimace. "Sure thing."

He reached out and gave her shoulder a quick squeeze before he strode off to the front counter. The feeling of his warm hand through the fabric of her thin blouse lingered. His fresh scent of sea salt and bergamot cologne was like a flash of tranquility in this stale place.

She watched as he approached the front counter and showed his badge once again, this time to a correctional officer in the same navy uniform as the one at the gate. From behind the safety partition familiar to all prison reception areas, the guard shook his head and said something she couldn't quite make out. Jake's response came loud, clear, and angry.

"What?" he snapped. "When did this happen?"

Again, the response was muffled.

"I want all the files on this, and I want them *now*."

She rose from her seat and made her way over to him. He turned, his face flushed, with a hard expression. The tenderness he'd shown her moments before had vanished.

"What's wrong?" He pursed his lips as if he didn't want to tell her. She inched closer and laid a hand on his forearm. "Tell me what's going on."

He let out a long breath and stepped away from the counter, his eyes full of fury. A quick staccato beat echoed off the walls as he paced back and forth the length of the waiting room for a moment before coming back to her. "There was a prison fight last night on the cell block where Freddy was held. He was killed. Our only suspect is dead."

****

Jake hated the wide-eyed stare of horror on Abby's face and instantly wanted to take back his words. But keeping the truth from her would only make matters worse. It wasn't that he'd never heard of prison fights or having a suspect killed. But this was too much of a coincidence. An ugly thought came into his head. Someone was keeping tabs on their whereabouts and maybe even tapping his phone. He had to get Kai to check it as soon as they got out of here. He balled his fists at his sides in frustration and drew in a series of shallow breaths. Another lead had bitten the dust.

She opened her mouth, then closed it again. Tears sprang up in her dark eyes, but she fought them back. "What do you mean, he's dead? Are you sure?" Her gaze darted from the prison guard to Jake and back again.

"Yes, ma'am," the officer answered. "I'm afraid so. Things like that don't often happen here, but I can't say they never do. This is a maximum-security facility. The worst offenders on the island are housed here. Because the prisoners are allowed to eat together, if you ask me, it's a powder keg waiting to happen—especially if the wrong inmates mix. It happened in the chow hall."

Jake nodded. "Someone shanked him in the neck with a sharpened toothbrush, but there was a crowd, so no one knows who did what. The warden and other correctional officials are still investigating. He bled out in a few minutes even before the ambulance could get here. He didn't stand a chance."

She folded her arms across her chest and paced the length of the counter. When she turned back to him, her eyes were wild like those of a feral cat. "Do you think this is a coincidence?"

Jake let out a long and slow breath and nodded a thanks to the guard. "No. Let's go sit down."

He put his arm around her and led her back to one of the metal chairs. She moved like a robot and didn't argue with him. He was afraid she was finally becoming overwhelmed with all that was going on. They were so close and then this. He was sure she'd seen difficult cases in her time, but this one was personal, which made every dead end that much more frustrating. After she was seated, he took the seat next to her.

"Should we go and see the warden?" she asked.

Jake knew the investigation was ongoing and they hadn't found anything out yet. "Not today. I'll follow up in a few days when they know more. The CO told me it's too early to have any concrete information right now. I know what a jolt this has been to you."

She put her head in her hands. "Once again, we've got nothing. Why does this keep happening? Why are they always one step ahead of us?"

He wished he had the answers that would erase all of her pain and frustration, but he didn't. Yet he did have cop instincts and a badge. And just a tiny bit of faith. Perhaps Abby was rubbing off on him after all. "Hang tight. I've got an idea."

****

It might have been a waste of time to speak to the warden until they figured out who did what, but Jake knew one person who might know something. Freddy's cellmate. Twenty minutes later, he was sitting in a stark windowless concrete room with only a table and two metal chairs bolted to the floor. A sharp turn of a key claimed Jake's attention, and he watched as a bearded guard escorted Craig Smithson into the room.

Tall and nearing retirement age, that was if criminals ever retired, this man had a haggard face and walked with a noticeable limp. His once dark hair was now peppered with gray, but his bright-blue eyes signaled alertness. And that was what Jake was counting on. His crimes consisted of mostly petty thefts until two years ago when he graduated to robbery with a deadly weapon. That's what landed him here.

The guard moved to secure Smithson's handcuffs to the table, but Jake waved him off. "I've got this."

The guard nodded and left the room as quickly as he had come in. The door banged shut, and a key slammed into the lock, securing the room from the outside.

"Mr. Smithson, I'm Lt. Jake Devereaux of the Hawaii Special Investigations Unit."

The prisoner narrowed his eyes at him. "Is this about the murder last night? I told the guards already I had nothing to do with it. I was down in the machine shop when it happened. Trying to get a trade skill so that when I get out in a few months, I can find a job. I don't want no trouble."

Jake clasped his hands in front of him on the table. This was all information he knew. But he was hoping the man could help him with something else. "I don't want trouble either. And you're not a suspect. But you were Freddy's cellmate, weren't you?"

He gave a slow nod. "He got here about six months ago and was quite a firecracker. So what do they do? Put him with the old guy to try and calm him down."

Jake raised an eyebrow. "Did it work?"

The man barked out a laugh. "I don't know. I guess. I got him playing cards instead of throwing punches most of the time, so I guess that's something. But I tell you, that kid had a chip on his shoulder the size of Maui."

This was new. But hardly a motive for murder. Jake rolled his hand in a gesture urging him to keep talking. "Oh yeah? About what?"

"That he shouldn't be in here. He bragged about a bunch of other crimes he committed and didn't get caught or tried for. He was madder than a hornet that this drug charge stuck and his daddy couldn't get him off like usual."

Jake nodded. Of what little he knew about Freddy, this all sounded about right. "What kind of crimes did he say he got away with?"

The man laughed again and then coughed. Jake slid him a glass of water he hadn't touched on his side of the table. After a beat and a few sips of water, Smithson got the cough under control. "That sounds pretty nasty. Have you had that looked at?"

Craig shook his head. "I'm on the list. Hey, do you think you can help me get checked out if I give you more information?"

Jake wasn't in the habit of doing favors for prisoners. But this man seemed sick, defeated, and forgotten. So perhaps he could help. Just this once. "I'll see what I can do. Tell me what you know."

Smithson nodded. "I guess it doesn't matter now, 'cause Freddy is already dead, and you can't throw any more charges at him. But he said he killed someone once and got paid a lot of money. He didn't get nailed for that, but he got caught for some drug charge. Karma, huh?"

Jake's pulse jumped a few beats. "Do you know who? Or when?"

"Some kid. A surfer. Said he got paid just to rough him up, but instead, the guy fought back, and he killed him. The person who hired him said it didn't matter, he'd gotten the job done. Freddy was proud of what he did, and I gotta admit, that scared me a little. I slept with one eye open most nights. No remorse from that one. None I saw anyways."

Jake leaned in. So Freddy was the killer. But he wasn't the brains behind Isaac's murder. "Did he say who hired him? And why?"

Craig shook his head. "No, man. And I didn't ask. The less you know in here, the better it is, know what I'm saying?"

This was the unspoken code in prison: mind your own business. Most of the cons he'd dealt with adhered to it. Nevertheless, it was something to go on. "I hear you. Would you be willing to testify about this? If it comes to that?"

Craig threw his hands up in the air, and his handcuffs jingled, jarring the quiet of the room and echoing off the bare walls. "If it helps me see the doctor quicker, sure thing. I owe you one."

"Thanks. I'll get that in the works. Is there anything else you remember, Freddy saying?"

He shook his head. "No. Just on and on about how he'd gotten away with a murder from like ten years back and still ended up in prison. I'd say, the streets of Hawaii and OCF are safer without him."

"Do you know who might have killed him?"

Craig laughed, which incited another coughing fit. Once he took another drink of water and recovered, he stared Jake straight in the eye. "Anyone, everyone, man. Freddy was too cocky, too higher than mighty. Thought he was better than anyone else here. That's the wrong attitude to have in prison. He made a lot of enemies. It could have been anyone. Or a group. I'm not sure. All I know is I bunked with Freddy and tried to get him on the right path, but I'm not a miracle worker, y'know?"

Jake let out a long breath. "I know, man."

Freddy Preston was now a dead end, but the one who organized the killing of Isaac was still out there. This thing wasn't over. Not by a long shot. Jake was more determined than ever to bring to justice the person behind his best friend's murder.

Chapter Ten

Eyes closed, Abby sat on the beach in the backyard of Jake's cottage, listening to the sounds of the waves rolling onto shore and then receding back to the sea. The last of the day's warm sunlight had begun to slip below the horizon. She scooped up handfuls of still heated sand in her fingertips and then let it flow out. As if by letting go of the sand, she was letting go of Jacob's words when she'd first come to the island: *this is a cold case—a dead end.*

Tears pricked the backs of her eyes, and she let them roll down her cheeks this time, unable to hold them at bay any longer. The killer of her brother was dead. She should feel something, a least a bit different. More at peace, maybe?

Jacob wanted to delve deeper to try and find out who was behind Isaac's murder and the threats made on her. He was adamant that person must be brought to justice. But she wasn't sure anymore if it even mattered. She'd come to the island thinking everything would change, but nothing had.

Her new cell phone beeped with a text message. She pulled it out to glance at the screen.

—you got what you wanted: your brother's killer. Leave the island. Or else—

Whomever was sending these threats, they wouldn't stop until she was off the island. Of course,

Jacob would try and find out who was behind these them, but she just wanted it over. Done with. She typed back a one-word reply.

—*okay*—

She stood and hurled the phone into the ocean. It skipped on the water like a flat rock, then splashed down a few feet out into the surf. It sank beneath the sea and vanished. She'd get a new one when she got back to New York. A truly new beginning if she didn't have any of the contacts she'd transferred over from her old phone. Right now, she didn't care. She sank down in the sand, and put her head between her knees, taking a few cleansing breaths. It felt good to get rid of the phone. At least until she wanted to make a call.

"A penny for your thoughts?"

She opened her eyes and found Jacob standing over her, a mug of fragrant herbal tea in each hand. He smiled a gorgeous grin and took a seat beside her on the sand. "Or is it a dollar, now? Or two? You know inflation gets me every time."

She smiled back as she accepted the hibiscus tea from him. The sweet smell of the flower along with lemongrass with a hint of apple floated up, and she inhaled deeply. The resulting exhalation began to relax her. Or was it the man sitting beside her that had done that?

"No need for money," she said. "I'll take the tea as payment."

He laughed. "That's good. I don't have any cash on me anyway. Who does anymore?"

She nodded. "I know what you mean. Our society is almost too busy to even deal with money and make change. It's always rush, rush, rush. And please tap your payment. Except here. This place is different."

He sipped his tea and gazed out onto the sky that was awash with orange, pink, and purple all melded together with the fading sun. The waves lapped in quiet rhythm onto the sand and back again as the water darkened with the receding light. She pulled her sweater around her as a cool breeze wafted over them, as if to say it was time to go inside. To go home.

"Yes, it is in many ways. And in many ways, it's the same as the mainland. But there's just something about this place. Even though I loved surfing from the moment I could walk, I never imagined I would live on an island with the ocean in my backyard."

She sighed. "Yes. The world works in mysterious ways sometimes, huh?"

He nodded and turned to her. "I left a message for Liko Ayoshi. His secretary said he was in California. He still loves to surf out there like we did back in the day when he's not busy defending his clients. I don't talk to him as often as I did when we worked together at the hotel, but he'll call me back soon when he knows it's important."

"That's good." She appreciated his willingness to keep going with the case, but for her, it was over.

"Kai got a lead on the car, but it was stolen from a high-end dealership yesterday morning, and the plates turned out to be fake. That's a dead end unfortunately, but we're still waiting on the fingerprints."

She nodded. "Okay."

"And I checked out the security tapes over at the hotel. Whomever ransacked your room was dressed as a handyman and gained access to your room with a master room key. He wore the standard uniform, so he didn't raise any suspicion, and security never flagged him. You can see him on the camera going in and then out carrying a box. He might be the same guy who grabbed you, but he had on a ball cap and glasses, so I didn't get a solid identification. I'm sorry. I know all of this isn't good news."

No, it wasn't. But it was what it was. She darted a glance in his direction, and found him staring at her, concern etched in his gaze. "What's wrong?" he asked. "I can see you've been crying. Is it because Freddy was another dead end? Because I'm not going to stop until I find out who was behind this. I promise you."

Reaching up, he brushed a stray tear from her cheek and let his fingers linger there for a moment. The warmth and strength of his hand made more tears surface. She'd gotten used to having him around. He was the closest thing she'd ever had to a relationship, to a family, but it was clear he didn't feel the same way about her as she felt for him. Not after he'd shrugged off their kiss. Besides, pretty soon, she'd be gone. Maybe they'd talk on the phone once in a while, but it would never be the same.

She gently pushed his hand away and swiped at her face with a rough hand. There was no point in telling him how she really felt. It would only create more awkwardness in their last moments together. "Yes, I guess so. I mean, I'm glad we found out who killed Isaac. In time, I think it will bring me peace. I don't really know how I imagined this ending, but it definitely wasn't like this."

"It's not over yet. We still need to find out who ordered the killing because Freddy was just a pawn. We're going to catch them. It's just a matter of time."

His handsome features were highlighted in the hazy glow of the evening. He looked like the Jacob she knew. The one she would have to say goodbye to tomorrow.

"I think I've had enough of this case. I just got a threatening text telling me to leave, and this time, I'm going to listen to it. I just threw the phone in the ocean. It's over. I appreciate all you did for me, more than you'll ever know. And now that I know who killed my brother, that's enough for me. I'm heading home in the morning."

He set down his tea in the sand and took her hand in his. "No. You can't leave yet."

This took her by surprise. She'd assumed he'd just accept her statement at face value. "Why not?"

He let out a long breath. "Because we haven't solved the case. And we still don't know who is behind the threats on you." He gazed out into the ocean. "I'll go find your phone. We can use it as evidence." When he moved to get up, she placed a firm hand on his arm and shook her head.

"No. Don't. It doesn't matter anymore. Whoever was threatening me won't bother me as soon as I leave the island and stop looking into this case. The case is the reason I got the threats in the first place, and once I'm gone, it will be over. Besides, I'm sure you want to get back to your life with your team. With your new family. You don't need me hanging around."

He squeezed her hand. "Hanging around with you has been the highlight of my week."

She laughed through her dried tears and pulled away from him. He was clearly joking with that comment. She had to get used to not being around him.

It felt too good to be holding his hand, and soon, it wouldn't be there. She'd be alone. As it was meant to be. "Thanks for the compliment, but I have to get going. I have work, New York, all that stuff."

"Stay. And I'm going to be completely honest with you this time. It's not about the case."

She turned to him. The sky was fading fast, and dark-violet clouds filled the sky. The palm trees in the distance appeared as stark black silhouettes. It was time to end this. But she'd let him say his piece at least. She fiddled with a button on her sweater. "If it's not about the case, then what is it about?"

"You and me."

Her heart skipped a beat as she stared into his brilliant blue gaze. Did he feel what she felt? Did he want something more than friendship? Had she read the signs all wrong?

****

Abby's face went from total surprise to a forced grin as he shared his news with her. It was clear something still bothered her. Perhaps she sensed he wasn't being completely honest. And getting another threat didn't help. But no matter what, it was truth time. Even if it drove her away, she deserved to know the truth. After she pulled her hand away, he picked up the still warm tea, though it was a poor substitute for the soft skin of her fingers. "I think it was fate you came here. And now, I have to be honest with you."

Her eyes remained full of the pain from news gained over the day. He wished he could erase it all from her beautiful face. In time, it would fade no doubt. There was no way he was able offer her more than friendship after what he'd done, and he was quite sure that was all she wanted anyway. Besides, her life was in New York, and the five-thousand-mile gap would only grow wider after they parted.

"Honest about what?"

"Honest about the hole I dug for myself when I first tried to solve Isaac's murder. I worked day and night, pretending I was living a normal life, but I was living a lie. One Tamara, my ex, called me on the day she walked out on me."

Those beautiful eyes narrowed on him. "What lie, Jacob? What did you do?"

"I drank. A lot. Day and night. I was an alcoholic. An addict just like my father. And like your mother. I told myself it wasn't as bad because it wasn't illegal drugs, but I was just kidding myself. The loss of my best friend, the obsession about the case, the fights with my ex, they were all just excuses I made for the drinking. In the end, I was no better than our parents."

She reached over and grabbed his hand. "You're not your father or my mother. I can promise you that."

He scoffed. "Oh, yes, I was. And I almost ruined my life here because of it. If it weren't for Benny, Grace, Kai, and the governor, I would probably be passed out somewhere right now with an empty bottle in my hand. They gave me my life back. Helped me recover and get back on my feet. I've been sober for over a year now. But I'm not ready for a relationship, and I probably never will be."

"I get it, and I feel the same about relationships," she said, a sad smile on her face. "They're amazing, this team of yours. Sometimes when our own family doesn't work out, we make our own. That's what you did. I'm so happy for you."

He cocked his head. There was something she wasn't saying. Perhaps, his worst fear had come true. She no longer respected him after what he'd told her.

"Thank you for telling me, for being honest with me. That takes a lot of courage."

He shook his head. "What it takes is honesty. And it's something I should have shared with you a long time ago. Will you stay? See this case through to the end?" If she said yes, maybe he had a chance. A chance to make amends and see if they had something because even though he'd just told her he wasn't ready for a relationship, something about her just wouldn't let him give up. But if she didn't want to stay, he'd have to let her go and make his peace with it.

She paused, then slowly shook her head. "I'm sorry. It's time for me to go."

"I understand." He did. In her own way, the journey was over for her. They weren't meant to be. But he wasn't going to stop. "I'm still going to find out who's behind the threats and bring them to justice."

"I know you will." Her smile was wide and genuine this time. She moved closer and tucked her legs up underneath her. Silence followed for another beat as they watched the last of the light leave the earth for another day.

"It's beautiful." Her voice was just above a whisper. But her serene words reached him. And brought him back to the surface of what he'd be missing when she left.

He turned and took in her profile in the light of the fading sky. She had let down her hair out of its tight knot, and it fell in waves of ebony down her shoulders and back. Her mouth was upturned into a small smile as she stared into the sunset. The semidarkness only served to highlight the delicate features of her face and neck. Sure, the sunset was nice, but she was the one who was beautiful.

"I think so, too," he murmured. She turned to him, her eyes blazing. He leaned in closer and smelled the sweet scent of floral notes from the tea, and his hunger to taste her once again flickered to life. And this time there was no fire extinguisher in sight.

As Abby's tongue darted out, Jacob captured it with his and pulled her in for a kiss. Her mouth crashed into his in a desperate attempt to get as close as two people could be. He tasted the vibrant currents of the tea with a hint of spice. Closing his eyes, he surrendered to her soft touch and feel.

She moaned into his mouth and deepened the kiss. Their tongues twirled in a tango of temptation. The heady scent of coconut and sunshine surrounded him, and he welcomed it. As he reached out a hand to stroke her glossy tresses, he sighed. There was no place he'd rather be. Despite what he'd just said about not being able to get close to anyone, with this sensuous woman in his arms, all of his troubles just melted away like the spring thaw on the mainland after a long hard winter.

****

Abby closed her eyes as all her inhibitions vanished into thin air as soon as Jacob's lips met hers. She lifted her hand and cupped his smooth cheek with her palm. Sexy as sin.

As their lips met again, this kiss was softer. Less urgent. But held a promise of the intimacy that was to come. Surrounded by his sea salt and bergamot scent and strong muscular arms, she had everything she had ever wanted. If only for tonight.

He lowered her to the sand, and she sank into its softness. Her hair fanned out around her, and she was glad she had let it loose. Free. To do what it wanted. She opened her eyes as he hovered over her, gazing at her with his mysterious dark look that still held many secrets. Secrets she might or might not ever know. But right now, she had all the information she needed.

"You are so beautiful."

She opened her mouth to say something, but no words came out. Instead, she took in the serious and sensuous man hovering above her who made her feel these intense emotions. Want. Need. Desire. They swirled around in her stomach like moths to a flame. Then they magically burst into a kaleidoscope of graceful butterflies in every color of the rainbow and took flight. She wanted to soar with them. With him. Up to the high heavens and then down the vast mountainside to a land of sea and sand where troubles washed away with the turning tide. Where everyone was happy. Content. Cherished.

"I want to make love to you." He leaned down and kissed the shell of her ear. His lips trailed down her neck and into the hollow of her collarbone as his hand wandered to her hip and closed around the waistband of her yoga pants. Her breath hitched as his hand moved upward and cupped the lace of her bra. He lingered there. Touching. Feeling. Igniting the heat coursing through her veins into a full-on five-alarm blaze. Desire was percolating between them. And it was about to be fulfilled.

She reached up and ran her fingers through his thick, dark hair. He leaned into her touch. She smoothed back the locks that had fallen into his eyes. Her fingers moved down to the soft cotton of his T-shirt. She felt the strong muscles of his chest through the fabric. Flawless. A longing she never knew she had whispered through her. Telling her this was right. This was perfect.

"I do, too." Her voice was a breathy whisper. So unlike her own. But it was the voice of a woman who knew what she wanted. If only this one time. And she was going to get it. She could tell from everything that had happened to him he wasn't about to start something. Neither was she. But they did have this precious time together to shut out the world and their troubles. At least until dawn.

"I want this. I want you." She raised her voice to be heard over the ocean surf. This was one night. That was something they could both agree on.

A slow provocative grin spread across his handsome features, and she felt the corners of her mouth turn up as well. His hand slid under her shirt and across the flat plane of her stomach. She shivered when his light touch tickled her belly.

His strong arms came around, and he pulled her into a warm embrace. She leaned her head on his shoulder as he rose from the sand, cradling her in his arms. As they moved away from the shore and down the beach toward the house, she thought she would feel a chill. But his warmth blanketed her, and she felt as if she were floating on a feather in his embrace. Her wish was coming true. If only for tonight. And in this moment, that was all that mattered.

Chapter Eleven

Abigail heaved a long sigh as she zipped up her suitcase and pulled it off the bed. Her gaze traveled around the luxurious guest room Jacob had given her. She had to admit, this room was breathtaking and perfect for her. It was more opulent than what she had at the Hawaiian Oasis Resort. A king-sized bed frame in done in dark cherry wood with intricate carved vines and leaves flowing in every direction took up the center of the room.

This was the place where she'd had one magical evening. Jacob had made love to her deep into the night right here, and then she'd slept in his arms like a princess who'd had all her dreams come true. He'd left the bed at dawn, murmuring about getting a jump start on the case and hadn't returned. That's when the fairy tale came to a screeching halt. It was never meant to be a permanent thing between them, no matter how hard she might have wanted it to be true.

Her fingers ran over the burnt orange and gold bedcovers, and she caught a glimpse of herself in the mirror by the door. Her body tingled at the memory of the firmness in his touch, the lush feeling of his lips. His pleasurable…everything. To the nth degree. Shaking off her shivers, she made her way to the mirror. Glancing at her reflection, she noticed something. She looked different. Oh sure, her hair was in its usual knot, and she wore the startled look of someone caught daydreaming on the job. But something else was evident. She appeared happy and content. Had Jake done that?

No, it would never work between them. He was happy here and said he didn't want a relationship. He was a friend. That was all. One-night stands were not her thing and never ever with someone she considered only a good friend. But then she reasoned with herself although this situation wasn't ideal, it was only meant to be a one-time thing. Nothing permanent. And they had already agreed to that, so that eased her guilty conscience. A little. Still, it didn't take away the waves of feelings that washed over her, and she wondered, what if?

She shook her head to clear her erratic thoughts and focused on the large, fluffy feline sleeping in the room. He stretched out, taking up half of the bed and snored a little in his sleep. She smiled over at Leo. The plush bedspreads must have been handspun from the finest materials. They weren't something he'd have picked out, she was sure, but they were pretty. She swung her suitcase over the edge of the bed, and her toes sank farther into a cushy silver rug at her feet.

The walls of the room were done in a calming coral, and there was a large dresser, mirror, and a wardrobe done in the same wood as the bed. As beautiful as it was, the crowning jewel of the room lay at the far end of the room. Large double glass doors leading onto an outdoor balcony and a view of the ocean. That's what she would miss most about this place. The beach. The ocean. And most of all Jacob. But there was no way she could stay here even if she wanted to. No. She needed to get back to her life in New York.

Well, this was it. She was packed and ready to go. The only thing she hadn't done was scatter her brother's and her mother's ashes, but she planned to do that with Jacob just before she left the house. She blew a kiss to a sleeping Leo, and then she heard Jacob out in the living room, talking on the phone. After putting on her high heels, she strode out in search of some caffeine and breakfast before her long flight back to the mainland. And hopefully none of the small talk that went with a one-night fling. She wasn't disappointed.

Jacob was seated at the wood dining table with his laptop and his phone plastered to his ear, facing away from her. He wore a blue-flowered Hawaiian shirt and black cargo pants, which might have been amusing to her if it weren't for the tight expression and scowl on his face. She didn't want to interrupt him and was pleased she didn't have to rummage in the kitchen to find something to eat and drink.

He'd laid out everything earlier. She poured a coffee from a thermos and took a blueberry muffin from the end of the table, then strode to the comfortable looking but stark white sofa. Being careful not to spill any of her food or coffee, she took a seat.

She supposed he'd been up for hours, judging from the row of coffee cups littered next to him, and was now getting briefed on the cases he'd missed while he'd been helping her. No matter. Soon she'd be out of his way, and he could go back to doing what he did best.

She glanced out the bay window onto the bright green lawn and dark sky. A storm was brewing. Gunmetal-gray clouds spread across the sky at a swift speed, and rain began to pelt the glass with a deafening roar. A flash of lightning lit up the sky in the distance. The morning had been bright and clear. Not a cloud in the cobalt sky, but it had changed quickly as she packed up her suitcase. This was her final day in Hawaii, and except for the day she'd arrived, it was, for the first time on her trip, raining. It was almost as if the weather didn't want her to leave. She had her doubts as well. But life must go on.

She just hoped her flight wouldn't be delayed. Pulling out the new cell phone that Jacob had left for her on her pillow this morning, she checked her airline reservation. Everything was on schedule. A nonstop flight from Honolulu to New York's JFK airport. Back to city life and snow again. She breathed out a long breath, then slipped it back into her jacket pocket.

She was dressed in a teal pantsuit today for the flight home. She planned on heading straight to the office when she got back, so she wanted to be prepared, and she would be if she worked on the flight the entire way home. It was a long road ahead, but she was ready. She leaned back, and she sipped her coffee while she waited for Jacob.

"Okay, good," she heard him say into his cell phone. "After you send me the information, I'll go over it." A pause ensued on the other end of the line.

"Really? Are you sure? I think you need to check again. That doesn't make sense. Just text me, and I'll look into it. Let's just keep it between us for now. Thanks, buddy. You gotta stop pulling these all-nighters."

Jake barked out a laugh. "Okay, I will. Talk to you later." He disconnected and turned toward her.

"Good morning," he said and crossed the room to join her on the sofa. His voice held a bit of tension. It had to be work. That was all.

"Hi," she said. "Everything okay?"

It wasn't okay. She didn't quite know why those words came out of her mouth. They'd just connected like a real couple in a loving relationship for a scant few hours, and now it was all over. Of course, they'd both agreed to it, but still. What was okay about that?

He shook his head. "Actually, no. I just got off the phone with Kai. He came across something strange in Freddy Preston's financial records."

She set down her coffee. Okay, so they'd talk business before pleasure. She could handle that. She leaned in toward him. "Oh yeah? What was it?"

He opened his mouth to answer, and his cell phone chimed in his hand again. He held up a finger. "Just a sec," he mouthed, then spoke into the phone in his gruff deep voice. "Devereaux."

She picked up her coffee again. At this rate, he might even be too busy to discuss what had happened last night or to go with her to scatter the ashes of her brother and mother. It was good. They didn't need an awkward goodbye hanging in the balance between them. Besides, she was capable of just going and pouring the ashes herself while she waited. It wasn't like it was a planned funeral or anything. She stood to go and retrieve the urns from the bedroom when Jacob's voice caught her ear.

"Rusty. Good to hear from you. What can I do for you?"

She paused and tried to listen in. Why would Rusty Collins call now?

"That is strange," Jake said. "Are you positive?"

She strained to hear the other end of the conversation, but it was a jumble. As she entered back into the room and watched him, she held her breath. "An argument? When was this?" His eyes narrowed as he made his way over to the dining room table and began jotting something down in his memo book. "Anything else?"

More mumbling. She peeked over his shoulder to see what he was writing, but she couldn't make it out. His emotions were about as easy to decipher as the chicken scratch he was writing down right now. But it didn't matter. Not anymore. Chances are, they'd lose touch within a month or sooner. It was just natural progression. Nothing more.

"That's solid information. Thank you for calling. Do you know what made you recall the information?"

Another pause. He rubbed his temples as if staving off a headache. She wanted to tell him to lay off the caffeine. The three or four cups he'd drank this morning couldn't be good for his nerves or his head.

"Okay. Hang tight, and I'll be right over to take your formal statement." He asked for an address and then hung up. He turned to her with a grim expression on his face.

"What is it?"

He let out a long sigh and rubbed the back of his neck. "You're not going to believe this. Heck, I'm not sure I even believe it myself."

She placed a hand on his forearm despite her recent promise to herself to keep her distance. "Did Rusty have some information?"

He opened his mouth to say something as a loud

crash sounded from the front of the house. The ear-splitting splintering of wood and shattering of glass jarred them both, and they froze in their tracks. A second later, heavy footsteps thundered down the hallway.

"What the—" Jake pushed her behind him and fingered his weapon.

Three masked men dressed head-to-toe in black army fatigues appeared in the living room before he could unholster his handgun. All pointed semiautomatic rifles at both of them. The guns were big, menacing, and Abby let out an involuntary scream.

"Shut up! And get down on the floor. Now!" While one of the black-clad men shouted at the top of his lungs, another one lunged toward Jacob, the third toward Abby. Jacob tried to draw his gun, but the other man was faster and knocked it out of his grip, then hit him with the butt of his rifle. A loud crack of bone against metal echoed in the large living room.

"Jacob!" She tried to get to him, but the man near her grabbed her and jammed the rifle into her side. Searing pain laced her abdomen, but she fought back the tears. When she opened her mouth to scream, he pulled a gag out of his pocket and stuffed it in her mouth, securing it with a roll of duct tape attached to his belt.

She stumbled when he pushed her to the floor. Her knees smacked hard on the hardwood floor with a crack, and she winced. Then he shoved her hands behind her back and pushed them together. She struggled, but it was no use. The man was a hulk and at least twice her size. She thought he was going to handcuff her, but instead, he rolled out more duct tape and tied it around her wrists several times. Tight. She squirmed but couldn't move a muscle. He had her.

Abby watched in horror as the other masked man tied up a limp Jacob. Chills of dread ran down her spine in rivulets of rain as she strained to get a look at the wound on the back of his head. His blood was splattered on the floor in bright-red droplets, and his eyes remained closed. That wasn't good.

"Don't worry, princess," the man beside her sneered as he grabbed the backs of her elbows and hauled her up off the floor into a standing position. She moved her legs okay, but she wasn't going anywhere.

"It's just a flesh wound," he taunted. "We aren't allowed to kill him. The big boss wants to do it this time. Make sure it's done right."

The big boss? This was what Jacob had been talking about before—at the prison.

He was her family. Even if she left this island and never saw him again, she now realized in her heart she'd never been alone. And the only thing she couldn't live with would be if something happened to him because of her. Because she hadn't left when she'd said she would.

"Got 'em?" the first man yelled.

"Yup," the other confirmed. The first man leaned into the radio clipped at his shoulder, training his weapon on both of them. The enormous firearms with their ominous black barrels capable of doing so much damage made her let out an involuntary shiver. And with this trigger-happy trio, there was no hope of escape in her current predicament of being covered with duct tape.

"We've got the packages," he said into the mike.

"Delivery in twenty minutes. All gift wrapped at your request. Over and out."

Abby gagged as she tried to scream, but her mouth was full of cloth. She drew in a deep breath through her nose and fought back the tears that stung the backs of her eyes. Theses masked cowards might end up killing her, but she wasn't going to let them see her cry.

"Let's go, Miss Star Reporter," the man beside her jeered as he pushed her with a rough hand toward the hallway. She pushed down on her feet, trying to dig her heels into the hardwood floor. When her captor noticed what she was doing, he kicked her knees out from behind her, and she fell to the floor with a loud smack. Her right shoulder smashed into the floor with a whack, and she cringed.

"Okay," he yelled. "We'll do it your way." He scooped her up in one move like she weighed no more than a ragdoll and carried her under one arm toward the front door. She looked over her shoulder to see that the other man was dragging a still unconscious Jacob.

As she stared up at her captor, her already frozen blood ran ice cold and seemed to clog in her veins. She held her breath and took a closer look. The man who was holding her hadn't removed his mask, but it didn't cover his neck, and right there, in black and white, she spied his tribal tattoo—the same black triangle with an intricate design and the initials. Only now, she could read it all. H.G.S. Her eidetic memory confirmed he was the one who had tried to abduct her at the police station. Only this time, it looked like he was about to succeed.

****

Jake groaned and opened his eyes. Rain pelted

down upon him like ice-cold daggers from the dark sky above. His soaked shirt and pants clung to his body, and his head ached like it had been stuck in a vise grip for a week. He struggled to bring his hands to his searing head, but they remained tied behind his back and wouldn't budge.

He tried to drag in a ragged breath over the roar of an engine and the torrential rain hitting him from all angles. He was on the wooden floor of some sort of boat that bumped and lurched in the rough seas. This wasn't a day for casual sailing, that was for sure. It could only mean one thing. Trouble. His memory came crashing back like a tidal wave. He remembered three thugs bursting into his house and losing his gun as he tried to draw it from the holster. After that, everything went black.

He bent his neck to wipe the rain off his face with his shirt—and when he did, it was streaked with blood. He couldn't have lost a lot since he was conscious, but that explained the headache and the lump he felt forming at the back of his skull. He forced his eyes into focus. The vessel wasn't massive but had an interior cabin where he guessed the masked men who brought him here were, and a deck on the back with white benches where he lay. There was nothing he spied that he could use to free himself. All of the supplies had been put away out of reach.

Abby! His mind flashed back to the house and one of the men pointing a semiautomatic at her head.

"Abigail!" he called out as he shuffled around to get a better look at his surroundings and search for her.

"Jacob!" she called back, and then he spotted her to his left. She lay beside him on the floor a few feet out of reach. Her beautiful suit was drenched with rainwater, and her hair was plastered to her face. He didn't see any visible injuries on her. But that didn't mean there weren't any.

"Are you hurt?"

"No," she called back. "I'm fine. They gagged me till we got on this boat, then I guess when they got out on the open water, they figured no one could hear us out here. The men have been inside most of the time. I haven't seen any other boats out here or anywhere we can call for help."

He shook his head, and it throbbed in protest. "No. No one's out here. Only a crazy person would be fool enough to take a boat out in this storm."

As if the sky heard his words, a crack of thunder boomed, followed by a streak of lightning that lit up the heavens like a Fourth of July fireworks display. The storm might end up swallowing them whole before the kidnappers even got to them. He pulled on his restraints again to no avail.

"Are you okay?"

"Yeah, I'm good." His splitting headache protested otherwise, but he needed to be strong. She was safe for now, but he needed to get her out of danger. He needed to find a way out of this. As he struggled to sit up, the boat pitched and heaved, throwing him face down back on the deck. When he rose a second time, he propped himself up against the side of one of the benches. He saw the three masked men inside the cabin of the boat. Dry and safe. All the while, they'd left them out and exposed to the elements. He narrowed his eyes to try and get a good look at the men as she shimmied over.

"One of the guys, he's the one who tried to kidnap

me at the police station. I recognized the tattoo on his neck. The other two, I don't know," she said as she slid beside him and leaned on him for support. "This time I saw all the initials. They were H.G.S. Do they sound familiar to you?"

They did, but with his aching head, he couldn't think straight. "I think so. Give me a minute; it'll come to me. I just gotta think."

She put her head on his shoulder, and he racked his brain. H.G.S. What did they mean? He took a deep inhale. Even after all the rain, he still smelled her coconut perfume on her skin. He needed her touch. He needed her. He had to get them to safety.

After he was silent for a few beats, she turned to him. "Do you know what's going on?" Her breath was uneasy and coming in short bursts. He sat up straighter, and she leaned on him farther and caught her breath.

"I'm beginning to piece it all together. But it still doesn't make much sense."

She gazed over, and for the first time since all of this happened, he saw something in her eyes. Something he hadn't seen after she'd been kidnapped, threatened, or gotten that alarming phone call. What he saw was fear. He had to fix this. Now.

"What do they want with us?" Her breathing slowed as he leaned his forehead against hers. She was safe for now, but it wouldn't last long.

He strained and stole another glance inside the cabin. The men touched shoulder to shoulder as the space wasn't big, but as he noticed them standing around, a familiar scene popped into his head. He'd seen them before. This whole thing finally made sense. It was all coming together. And not in a good way. But he wasn't going to lie to her in order to try and protect her. He wasn't that man anymore. Besides, both of their lives were on the line. She deserved the truth.

"They want to kill us."

Chapter Twelve

The rain was slowing, but the sky still held ominous dark clouds as the boat pulled into a deserted industrial section on the other side of the island. She knew they'd not traveled long so was reasonably sure they were still on Oahu. "Why do they want to kill us, and where are we? If they'd wanted to off us, they could have done it back at your house." She dragged herself away from Jake to hide the fact they'd been talking from their captors.

She watched them as she had been leaning on his shoulder and breathing in his familiar and comforting sea salt and bergamot scent. They seemed more concerned about sharing a cigarette before they killed them. The stale smell of smoke emanated from the small cabin to the right of them.

"We're still on the island," he confirmed. "Just over on the other side. Nothing in this part of town but a shipyard and a few old canning factories. Most are abandoned. I suspect we're going over there. These men were ordered to bring us here. Alive."

He jerked his head in the direction of a large, dilapidated warehouse. She strained her neck to see better where he was pointing. White paint was peeled off the gray structure; an enormous wooden sign, faded and unreadable, hung off one side. She leaned over and soaked her bound wrists in a puddle of water that had formed on the deck. The tape was tight. But it wasn't entirely waterproof. If she got it wet enough, she might be able to loosen it.

The engine rattled, let out a tap, tap, tap, then died. The air around them became eerily silent. They cruised toward a dock that had definitely seen better days. It was missing a railing and a bunch of floorboards. The boards that remained in place hung from large rusty nails and looked like they might drop at any second.

"Why? What's going on? Freddy is dead, and he's the one who murdered my brother. Why are they still after us? Do you think it was his hotshot lawyer father who contracted these masked men? I heard them talking about a big boss. But I don't understand. Why would it matter now?"

He shook his head. "It's not about Freddy. Not anymore. He was just a hired gun like these guys are. They're—"

The door to the cabin slammed open so hard it bounced off its hinges. The men piled out one by one, bringing the strong stench of just-smoked cigarettes with them.

"Well, looky here. Jakey boy is awake," one of them said. "Did you have a nice nap, lieutenant? Because you're about to have another one. But this one is going to be permanent."

Another man lurched forward and hauled Jacob up onto his feet. Abigail saw him wince, but he didn't struggle. Did he have another plan, one that he hadn't had time to tell her about?

"Look, man," Jake said as he straightened. "Just let the girl go, okay? She's got nothing to do with this. It's all on me."

The man barked out a laugh and turned to his comrades. "Do you believe this guy?"

They laughed as if they were in on some private joke. "She's the one that started this whole mess."

"Yeah," another man agreed.

"There's no way she's getting out of this. And neither are you. The big boss says both of you are to be delivered. So that's what we're going to do."

Jacob jerked away, but the man grabbed him and slammed a fist into his gut. He doubled over but rose again in a quick and flurried motion.

The second man grabbed Abigail and hoisted her to her feet. He drew a knife from his belt and held it against her throat. She didn't dare struggle now, and Jacob froze in his tracks.

"Easy, Jakey," he said. "You wouldn't want something to happen to the lady too early because you need to play cop, do you?"

Fury burned bright blue in Jacob's gaze, but he didn't say another word or struggle as their captives led them off the boat and down the creaky dock. At the end of the pier, they were shoved onto a path that ended at the warehouse Jacob had indicated earlier.

The place was deserted. She looked to and fro, but didn't see a soul. There were no other boats or cars around. The air held the crisp scent of freshly washed rain, but she was quite sure nothing could clean this place. Except for maybe a bulldozer and a wrecking ball. It reeked of death and destruction. This was one of the forgotten places on the island and a site where she very well might draw her last breath. Worry snaked through her like a slithering reptile. Would Jacob be able to tell her what this was all about before it was too late? Or would she go to her grave, wondering?

Weeds and tall grass grew among the cracks in the asphalt, and she stumbled now that she was missing a heel that had broken off from one of her shoes. It had cracked and separated from her shoe while she was trying to jam it into the floor back at the cottage in an attempt to stall the men.

She used this to her advantage and took a chance. Falling backward, she landed hard on the pavement littered with sharp pieces of broken glass from beer bottles. One shard bit into her shoulder, but she clenched her teeth to keep from crying out. She quickly palmed a pointed piece and closed her hand over it. Now she had a weapon.

The man rolled his eyes and grabbed her arm.

"Stop. I'm hurt," she pleaded.

Jacob's gaze flashed to hers, and she nodded ever so slightly to let him know she was okay and that she was faking it.

"Let's go, lady," the masked man taunted and heaved her onto her feet. He wasn't the one who tried to abduct her at the police station, but he was just as nasty. The jacket of her pantsuit ripped as he pulled on her arm. "Don't want to miss the show, do you?"

She felt her forehead crinkle in concentration as she stared up at the man. What was he saying now? "What show? What are you talking about?"

The man jabbed a beefy finger in Jacob's direction. "The show where your boy here gets executed. And you get to watch. Then guess what?"

She didn't want to guess. Pursing her lips together, she remained silent. He jabbed her in the ribs where earlier he'd hit her with the butt of his gun. Pain flared in her side, but she stamped it down.

"Guess what?" he repeated.

"What?" Her mumble was barely above a whisper.

"You're next."

****

Jake looked over at Abby as the men abandoned their masks before congregating in a far corner of the warehouse, no doubt to contact the linchpin of this whole operation. With their masks off and their faces showing, it was pretty clear they no longer saw Abby or him as a threat. Both of them would be dead if they didn't get out of here soon. Because, as everyone knows, dead men or women don't talk. Jake had some clear evidence to the contrary but would never get the chance to show it in court if he didn't get himself and Abby free.

They were both tied to metal chairs in the middle of a vast space with a cracked concrete floor beneath their feet. If he could just free himself enough to get his hands on a piece of broken rubble, he'd have a weapon to try to use against the thugs.

Many years ago, this place was used as a pineapple factory, but was abandoned after it was discovered growing pineapples was too expensive in Hawaii. Another tradition the Hawaiian people had lost, along with thousands of jobs. Now, it lay empty except for a few pieces of metal equipment lying around.

He knew the history of this place, including quite a few bids to build homes or hotels on this site, that always seemed to fall through at the last minute. In the meantime, this area had become a hotbed for criminal activity. He and his team had raided this area many times. He'd just never realized that one day, he'd have to escape this place.

Grime covered windows at the top of the building allowed dull light into the place, but they were too high to climb up and escape. That left the cracked glass door they'd come into on the left, or the industrial garage door to the right. First things first. He had to free himself. And Abby.

"Jacob," she whispered.

His gaze darted over to the men buried deep in conversation and then back to her. When she jerked her head back, he saw that she'd loosened the duct tape around her wrists enough to be close to freeing them. In one hand, she held a shard of green glass that she'd used to cut the tape. So that's what she'd been up to when she fell. It meant they had an edge, though only a slight one.

"Hang on," he whispered back. "Not yet."

She nodded, and he worked on his restraints. The torrential rain had loosened the duct tape, so it was no longer waterproof, which Abby had probably already surmised. He bent his wrists back and forth and stretched the tape out. Almost there.

Cheers and slaps resounded in the air and echoed off the empty walls and high ceiling. The men high fived each other like they were some sort of junior baseball team. Jake glanced over at Abby, and she fired him a questioning glance.

Once he'd gotten a good look at their unmasked faces, he knew what he'd suspected was true. The three men were locals with dark eyes and military buzz cuts. He knew what H.G.S. stood for. In fact, he knew they all had the same tattoo, but the only visible one was the guy who had it on his neck. He was sure they were the ones behind the notes, phone call, attempted kidnapping, and ransacking of the hotel room. And he now knew why their prints weren't in the database, although once again they were just dealing with the middlemen. But before he could tell Abby to be careful or any more information, the men broke up their little celebration.

"And without further ado." The man Jake knew as Marco he strode toward them. "Our guest of honor is here. Let the games begin."

Another man whom Jake knew as Brian trailed after him as the third one, Sam, went to escort the so-called *guest*.

"You're not going to get away with this," Jacob said. "If you give yourselves up right now, I'll put in a good word for you at the justice department."

Marco scoffed. "Your word is nothing. We are going to get away with this."

"Yes, we are," Brian taunted. "And we're going to be paid a huge wad of cash."

Jake had hoped these men, ones he'd viewed as men of honor at one time, wouldn't be fooled by the promise of money—or a pretty face.

But they had been. And so had he.

A sharp clicking of heels interrupted his thoughts as a petite woman in a long black trench coat strode toward them. She pulled off a black fedora and dark glasses, then handed them off to Sam.

Sam, Brian, and Marco: members of the H.G.S. or Hawaii Governor's Security.

The woman was Melinda Ayoshi, the Governor of Hawaii—and Jake's boss.

Chapter Thirteen

Abby looked from Jacob to the governor and back again. This made no sense. His boss, the governor of Hawaii, was behind the murder of her brother? She recognized her at once from the research she'd done before she'd arrived on Oahu.

Melinda Ayoshi was barely five feet tall, but what she lacked in stature she made up in presence. Her face was expertly made up, complete with bold black eyeliner and eye-catching red lipstick. Dark hair cut into a sleek bob made her appear powerful, yet approachable. Born into a wealthy family, a successful lawyer who then went on to become a prominent member of the government. What could she possibly have to do with murdering Isaac?

Governor Ayoshi sauntered over, a warm smile on her face like she was greeting them at a tea party. Her henchmen trailed after her like puppies, nipping at her heels and waiting for instructions to do her bidding.

She pulled a small handgun out of her coat pocket and aimed it first at Jacob and then Abigail. Abby recognized it as a designer special edition, 9mm, amethyst design that held seven in the chamber. Enough to kill both of them with a few to spare. She'd almost bought one for herself when she'd first moved to New York but then decided against it. Guns were a risky business. She'd taken a self-defense class instead.

Melinda obviously didn't share her dislike of firearms.

"Jake, Abigail. I see you both made it here in one piece." She laughed at her own joke as she no doubt took in his blood-stained shirt and her ripped pantsuit. Not a hair was out of place on her, nor was her heavy makeup smudged. Abby wondered how she managed to pull that off in the middle of a fierce storm.

"Melinda," Jacob said. "Turn yourself in now, before it's too late. You've done enough damage."

A shrill snarl escaped her lips. "On the contrary, I'm just getting started. And just so you know, this is all your fault."

Abigail shot a look at him, but he was busy staring down his boss. He arched a bloody brow at her. "What are you talking about?"

She let out a long sigh as if she were already bored. "If you had stayed the drunk, useless, and broken lieutenant I had hired for my task force, this never would have happened. But then you had to go and clean up yourself, making a name for your team. Keep your friends close, but your enemies closer, right? After you finally gave up looking into Isaac Hasting's case, though I was sure you wouldn't solve it, I still kept an eye on you. And then you go helping this reporter here—" She jabbed a perfectly manicured scarlet-red nail in Abby's direction. "—try and solve the cold case murder of her loser nobody brother from the mainland."

Jacob shook his head. "Only Isaac wasn't a loser. Or a nobody. He was good enough to win the surfing competition against your son Liko. Is that what this is about? You killed an innocent kid over a surfing contest. That's low. Even for you."

It now dawned on Abby that the box of Isaac's

things she'd brought with her had helped Jacob piece together the murder. She'd been the first to alert him about the surfing competition that he hadn't known Isaac had entered. Now, she just needed a little more help to get them out of this mess.

Melinda pursed her ruby-red lips as if she weren't sure she wanted to answer that question. "I probably shouldn't say another word. But I'm going to. Because soon you'll both be dead, and my other bodyguards are taking care of your precious team. Such a shame they got blown up in a drug sting gone bad the same day their lieutenant went missing after taking a boat out. The fish won't tell anyone where you are. They'll just feed on you."

Jake scoffed. "Enough with the dramatics, Melinda. This explains why you pay for security out of your own pocket. Of course, you always had security growing up to protect your wealthy banker father, so I guess it's just natural for you. Although none of the other governors have half the security detail you do. Some don't have any. It's insurance, I guess, for when you go on a murdering spree and need someone to clean up your mess. Is that what they did? They're all the muscle, and you're the brains of the operation."

She shrugged. "Now who's being dramatic?"

Jake shook his head. "I know what you did. I just don't know why."

For one long moment, she steepled her hands in front of her, then released them with one snap of her fingers. Marco materialized at her side and put out a chair for her. This one was white and padded. It appeared new and comfortable. Abby surmised this woman didn't know the meaning of traveling light. And apparently, this was going to be a long story, and she was getting comfortable.

"Jake, all you had to do was put her—" She jerked her head in Abby's direction. "—on a plane and send her back to where she came from. You even told me as much. When you didn't, I had to get creative with an attempted kidnapping and a few threatening phone calls. I'm a busy woman. I don't have time for this."

"Cut it out," Jake snapped. "Abigail deserves to know why a woman sworn to protect the country would do something like this. I know what you wanted with me now, but what about Isaac?"

She waved a hand at him. "Fine, fine. A last dying wish if you will. I'll indulge you. And her." Melinda indicated Abby again but refused to look her in the eye.

Interesting. Perhaps this woman wasn't used to doing her own dirty work. If Abby got half a chance, she'd make her pay. With a broken piece of glass if it came to that. She bit down on her lip and clutched the shard tighter in her palm.

Melinda crossed her legs in front of her and leaned over. Just out of reach. "Here's the thing. Before I was a governor or even a lawyer, I was something else. Do you know what that was?"

Jake tilted his head toward her. "A class-A manipulator?"

She shrugged and waved her gun around. As if she were annoyed with him and just might shoot him any second. "If need be. But no. What I was, was a mother. Now, I know you don't know a lot about that since you didn't have one, but mothers care. That is ones that don't die in childbirth and leave their sons with drug-addicted fathers. Most mothers care about their children. They care so much they would do anything for them. That was me. It still is. Liko and Isaac were head-to-head in the World's Pro Surfing Competition. No one could predict a clear winner. And Liko needed to win, wanted to win. He was a local, a true Hawaiian, and fast becoming a surfing legend. At the time, I was still a stay-at-home mother so my son was my entire life. I never thought I'd go on to law school or even governor, so what did I have to lose, right? And I couldn't let some nobody from nowhere Michigan take that away from him."

"Does Liko know about this?"

She put a hand to her heart while the other one held the gun by her side. "Of course not. I never tell him anything that will upset him. He's a sensitive child. Besides, mothers protect their children. They don't need to know all of the details, now do they?"

Jacob shook his head. "So when bribing Isaac didn't work, you opted for murder?"

She narrowed her eyes. "What do you know about a bribe?"

Jake laughed. "An anonymous source."

She scoffed. "Oh, that nosy surfing instructor Rusty Collins. Always in everybody's business but his own. I saw him the day I went to give Isaac a peaceful way out of this situation, but I couldn't be sure if he overheard my conversation. You see, if Isaac had just agreed to take the money from me, none of this would have happened. But he didn't, and it did. And now, there's another loose end I need to tie up. I tell you, a woman's work is never done."

"Marco," she called out. "Get someone to take out Rusty Collins. Make it look like an accident."

Marco saluted her. "Yes, ma'am. Right away."

She turned back to Jacob. "Now, where was I? Yes and no. I couldn't allow Isaac to win, but I also didn't mean to have him killed. After Isaac refused the payout, I hired Freddy to rough him up, just enough so he wouldn't be able to compete. How did I know the silly child had a strong streak to fight back once again, and Freddy would end up killing him?"

Melinda continued. "Sheesh, do they feed their children a dose of aggressive defiance with their breakfast cereal back in Michigan? Who knows? This kid didn't follow my rules, any of them. Unlike my precious Liko. He's a good boy. Anyways, it doesn't matter now. It wasn't my fault that he died, and as you know now from your little road trip to the prison, in the end, Freddy got what he deserved. Another job I had to organize. I'm telling you, it's a wonder I even have time to keep up with my manicures." She picked at a nail as the gun twirled around on her thumb.

Abigail bit her tongue, trying to hold back her emotions. But the sheer narcissism radiating off this woman overwhelmed her. She could add award-winning actress to her list of accomplishments. From what Jacob said, and the interview clips she'd seen of this woman, no one knew the real Melinda Ayoshi. Not even her own son. In all of the years of investigating cold cases and reporting on murders, Abby had never met a woman as sinful as her.

Abigail cleared her throat, and the governor glanced over at her in surprise. As if she'd almost forgotten Abby was there. "You killed Freddy, too? My, my, Governor, you've got a lot of blood on your hands. Aren't you worried it might not wash off before tonight's dinner party?"

****

Jake saw Abby deliberately antagonizing Melinda with her words, so much so he was afraid she was ready to make a move. He hadn't entirely loosened the duct tape keeping his hands tied together. He squirmed in his seat, and the last of the tape broke free. He worked quickly on the ropes tying them to the chair to try and work the knots loose with his hands. It wouldn't be as fast as Abby's piece of glass, but he'd had lots of practice with this sort of thing over the years.

Melinda laughed, but her eyes were dark pinpricks, and she held the gun pointedly at Abby now. "Oh, dear. You got the Michigan defiance too, I see. But to answer your question, no. I won't have blood on my hands, and my next event will be a funeral. To say goodbye to the dedicated members of my task force. What a tragedy to have them all die in one day."

She stood and pretended to wipe tears from her eyes. "I'll have to prepare a moving speech that will tug at the heartstrings of my people and urge stiffer penalties for drug crimes. But first things first. I have to kill both of you. Who wants to go first?"

"I do." Jake forced the governor's attention back with his words.

The knots were loose enough he figured he had a fifty-fifty chance of being able to get up out of this chair and make his move. It was the best it was going to get. He'd take it.

The governor cooed. "Oh, how noble of you to volunteer, and who am I to argue?"

She took a few steps toward Jake and aimed her bright purple gun at his chest. He guessed she wasn't a great shot if she needed to get this close. In fact, he was counting on that to be true. And if there was any justice left in this world, he wouldn't get taken out for good by a neon-colored firearm. That wasn't right, no matter how you sliced it.

A loud crash sounded outside, and a fiery explosion lit up the grimy windows, filling them with black smoke and red-and-orange flames. Another boom shook the old building right down to its foundation and reverberated off the concrete walls.

"It's our boat," Marco called as he rushed to the cracked window on the door to look out. "It's on fire and the dock is destroyed!"

Melinda scowled at Jake. "Do you know anything about this?"

Jake cocked his head at her. "I've been tied up here this whole time. So, no, you can't pin this on me. As much as I'm sure you want to."

The governor turned to her bodyguards. "Marco, go with Sam and check it out. Brian and I will take care of these two."

Brian stepped up as if he'd been summoned by the queen. Jake wouldn't have been the least bit surprised if he bowed down to her or something crazy like that. She had them wrapped around her little finger. It was her charm, her grace, and her pure evil. He'd been a victim once too, and he'd almost fallen for her plan. Almost didn't get his life together. But he did. He wasn't the broken man she'd hired a couple of years ago. Jacob Devereaux had changed, and he felt it in his soul.

Marco and Sam took off running. Their heavy boots slapped the pavement as they rushed out the side door. Melinda took another step toward Jake. It was now…or never.

He leaped out of the chair and lunged at Melinda with all of his might. She got a shot off, and his shoulder stung like a hundred bumblebees were attacking it, but he just kept coming. He knocked the smoking gun out of her hand, and it skittered to the floor and slid a few feet away. Brian aimed his semiautomatic at Abby's chair. Except she wasn't there anymore.

She was up and threw the piece of glass at Brian, striking him in the eye, and he cried out. Abby and Melinda scrambled for the gun. Jake tackled Melinda and knocked her to the floor, then like a quarterback trying to get his ball to the goal line, he dove for the next obstacle in his way.

Abby retrieved the gun and aimed it right at the governor's head. Brian froze in his tracks, as if unable to move at the thought of his boss being hurt. Blood gushed down his face from his injured eye, and he clasped one hand over it as Jake closed in on him.

"Governor Ayoshi," he called out.

"Shoot them, you idiot," she fired back, but Abby was upon her and held one arm firmly around her neck. The gun was jammed into the side of Melinda's head.

Abby shook her head. "I wouldn't move if you don't want her to die."

Chapter Fourteen

That was the split-second Jake needed. Adrenaline hummed in his veins, and he pounced on the bodyguard and tackled him the ground. As Jake struggled to free the weapon from Brian's grasp, the gun fired a few wild rounds. The bullets zinged into the air, and a rat-a-tat tapping sound echoed off the walls. One of the high windows smashed and rained down glass on them. The others lodged into the floor of the warehouse.

Jake got control of the gun and flipped it around. Grabbing the butt, he struck Brian in the forehead. The man crashed to the floor, going down like a ton of bricks and was out cold. Good. Jake didn't want to be the only one with a headache today.

His gaze zipped back over to Abby. "Are you okay? Did you get hit?"

She shook her head. "No. And neither did she."

"Good."

Jake abandoned the limp bodyguard and took control of a struggling Melinda as Abby backed away, still training the governor's own gun on her.

"You won't get away with this," she yelled. "My son, the lawyer, will get me off on the charges, and then I'll send you to jail for assaulting a member of the government."

Jake shook his head. "I don't think so. Liko won't want anything to do with you after he finds out what you've done. You've lost, Melinda. Your career, your family, and your dignity. I won't stop until I know that you'll spend the rest of your life behind bars."

She snarled at him and then fell silent. All her earlier bravado erased as evidenced from her tight lips and ashen face. After all of this time, her best-laid plans had blown up in her face, and Jake and Abby had been the ones to make that happen.

"Shouldn't you read Melinda her Miranda rights?" Abby asked. "After all, as governor even she isn't above the law."

"I'd love to," he replied. Grabbing a rope from the floor, he moved her hands around to her back. He wound it tight a couple of times in lieu of handcuffs.

"Governor Melinda Ayoshi. You are under arrest for conspiracy to commit murder and for the murder of Isaac Hastings. You have the right to remain silent. Anything you say can and will be used against you in a court of law."

As Jake finished reciting the standard warning, Melinda remained silent. Although he was disappointed that he hadn't caught on to the governor's game earlier, in his heart, this had been the right time. He'd done a lot of good work on the task force even with an evil boss at the helm and planned to do more in the future. He was ready.

The big metal garage door to the right suddenly burst down with a thundering crash, and in flooded a police SUV and two Honolulu Police Department sedans with their lights and sirens blaring and flashing. They screeched to a halt, tires smoking right in front of Jake, Abby, and Melinda. Melinda's wide eyes gave her a deer in the headlights look. It was over for her. She'd never hurt another person ever again.

Heavily armed police personnel in dark uniforms and Kevlar vests burst out of the vehicles, including the members of his team, Benny, Grace, and Kai.

"Is everyone all right?" Benny he ran toward Jake and Abby, Grace and Kai were right on his heels.

Jake nodded. "Yeah, we're fine. Nothing a week at the beach couldn't cure. But what about you guys?"

"Right as rain, brother," Kai said.

Jake turned to Abby. "Are you okay?"

He smiled over for the first time today, and she returned his warm gaze. Her tired eyes held a light in them he hadn't noticed before. Perhaps getting to the bottom of this case despite all of what they'd been through today had brought her the peace she'd so dearly desired. He hoped so.

Abby turned to Benny. "Yes. We're good, thanks."

"That's a relief." Grace approached with Kai in tow. With a rifle slung over one shoulder, she holstered her handgun before she enveloped Abby in a warm hug.

"We were so worried about you guys," she said. "Kai and I stopped by the cottage after our shift and found it turned inside out. We immediately called Benny and the HPD. Apparently, the governor was trying to call us in on a drug bust at the same time. The guys from the bomb squad were free and filled in for us and thank the goodness because it was a trap. No drugs, only a bomb which they diffused. We need to add that to her list of charges."

Kai nodded. "Yes, that and threatening a witness. Rusty Collins came to the station while we were moving out. He got a threatening call and decided to meet you at HQ. He's there now and will be under police protection until all this mess is sorted out."

"That's good," Jake said.

Kai cuffed the still silent governor with handcuffs from his belt and looked over at them.

"You read the gov her rights?"

"Yup," Jake confirmed. "Do me a favor, Kai, and get her out of here. I can't stand to look at her lying face for one more second."

"You got it, LT. Let's go."

Kai and one of the other HPD officers escorted the governor to a waiting police car and placed her in the back seat. In a couple of seconds, it was roaring off toward HQ, where she'd be printed, booked, and housed in a cell. Another two officers hauled up a bleeding Brian and put him into an ambulance that had arrived on the scene.

"Gee, I bet the governor is wishing she went ahead with those plans to reform the prisons, now that she's going to be their newest inmate." Benny laughed, and they all joined in.

Jake gave a half shrug. "I'm kinda glad she didn't. Now she's going to see firsthand what it's like inside Oahu Correctional. Hopefully, for the rest of her life."

Grace took a call from her cell phone and then turned back to the group.

"That was Sgt. Smith. They nabbed the two other bodyguards trying to escape in a leaky canoe. They'll be booked along with the governor. All four of them will go down for this. I imagine Brian, Sam, and Marco's fingerprints will match the ones in the car and at Abby's hotel."

"Yes," Jake said. "They Miranda's orders and did her bidding all along. It's finally over."

"Good," Abby said as tears filled her eyes and began to roll down her cheeks. Jake put his arm around her and pulled her close before he stopped himself. He wiped away her tears with a tender thumb, and Grace handed her some tissues.

"It's over. We did it." He hugged her close, and she clung to him. The stress of the day taking its toll. She was as strong and brave as they came, but even the brave and strong need a shoulder to lean on. He promised himself he'd be that shoulder for her as long as she needed it.

****

"How did you find us?" Abby asked as the scene started to calm down. She blew her nose and wiped away her tears with the tissues Grace had given her. Most of the police had holstered their weapons and were making calls and notes. A forensic team swept in to survey the scene. It was still loud, and her head ached with the ebbing of adrenaline flooding out of her system, but they were unharmed and safe. The person who wanted Isaac dead was arrested.

Jacob tightened his hold on her, and she leaned onto his chest for support. The comfort of his strong arms and the soothing beating of his heart lulled her into a state of calm, peace, and happiness for the first time since this journey began. She reveled in it. Even if it was for only just a moment.

"You weren't too hard to track down," Grace said. "As soon as we knew something was wrong, we activated the GPS signal in Jake's watch." Grace signaled for a standby police officer to bring Abby and Jacob some water.

Abby accepted a bottle and unscrewed the cap,

taking a long cold drink. Her dry throat was quenched, and her pulse was finally returning to normal after being sky-high most of the day.

"So," Benny said. "Who suspected the governor? Or was it a big surprise to everyone but me?"

They laughed, but then Grace became serious. "Kai knew something was off with the governor after he checked into Freddy Preston's financial records. Apparently, she wasn't too careful ten years ago and had paid him a large sum of money around the time of Isaac's murder. Kai did his magic computer work and uncovered evidence of the check. He told Jake this morning on the phone."

Jacob nodded. "Yes, he did. I thought it was strange, but we agreed to keep it between ourselves until I had a chance to look into it. But then I remembered the surfing competition that I discovered Liko won, and it was the same one Isaac was registered to but never attended. I wondered if Liko was involved. But he didn't have a clue. I'll have to call him later to fill him in and get a statement from him. He'd always mentioned back in the day his mother had some issues, but I didn't press him for exactly what. Little did he know too, I guess."

A chorus of agreement rose between the group.

"She was a good boss," Benny said. "But there was always something about her that I didn't quite trust. Guess I need to listen to my cop intuition next time."

"We all do," Grace agreed. "She had the people of Hawaii fooled with her fake charm and designer shoes. What other evidence do we have on her?"

Jacob cleared his throat and took a drink of water. "We have the witness Rusty Collins who called me this morning before all this happened. Said he saw the governor on breakfast television giving a speech about opening a new food bank when he woke up today. He remembered it was her who Isaac had been arguing with. Back then, we knew her, but not well. That's probably why he forgot about her. Lucky for us, he remembered. I was heading over to take his statement when we got grabbed by Melinda's bodyguards."

Despite her aching head, it all made sense to Abigail. It was true what Jacob had said earlier. Isaac had been an innocent kid and had gotten caught up in the greed of a mother, giving her son everything he ever wanted, at any expense. Even human life. It wasn't the way she'd imagined this turning out, but that's what had happened, and she was ready to accept it. Her brother's decade-old murder could now be put to rest.

It was time to go back to the mainland and begin her life anew.

Chapter Fifteen

Two days later, both Abby and Jacob received clean bills of health and some much-needed rest and relaxation. Jacob's shoulder wound turned out to be a graze, and a few stitches closed up the gash. Then he went back to work again. He'd been working on the case day and night, so she wasn't sure how much rest he was getting.

Abigail, on the other hand, had finally given in to some rest and relaxation. She'd taken one last advantage of the beautiful beach and warm sun as she planned out what to do when she got home. She wasn't sure investigative reporting was the job for her anymore, and she'd even jotted down some notes about ideas for a novel. It was a small start on the road to getting her life back, but an important one. She vowed to make her life full again, one without murder and violence. That she knew for sure. Peace had come to her on the island of Oahu.

They hadn't really talked about their one night together, and it was probably for the best. It would only make an awkward situation even more awkward. It was a fleeting moment. A passionate wrinkle in time. Now the only thing she had left to do before she went back to New York City was to scatter Isaac and her mother Akela's ashes out in the ocean. Then she'd drive to the airport and fly home. This chapter in her life was over, and it was time to move on, but this time with harmony in her heart.

She pulled a bright-yellow rash guard over her fuchsia swimsuit. Wearing bright colors reminded her that this final act was a celebration of the life her brother and mother had lived, not a mournful goodbye. She missed them dearly, but it had been their time to go. It helped to remember that.

Jacob had said he'd be home in a few hours to paddle out into the ocean with her, but he'd gotten stuck at the office and had sent her a text telling her he would be home later. All of the fallout from the governor's arrest and the impending case against her was taking up all of his time and then some. She didn't fault him for that. He was doing his job, what he loved, and he had a family, a life here. One she wasn't meant to be a part of.

It gave her great comfort to know she'd had a small part in helping him restore his life. She could leave knowing he'd be okay. If it had meant to be more than just friendship with him, as she'd thought in her heart at one time, it would have happened. But it hadn't, and it just wasn't meant to be.

She wandered out of the spare bedroom and down the hall to the living room with an urn in each hand. Leo appeared in the hallway and padded over. She set the containers down and patted the soft fur of the feline as he rubbed up against her leg. He purred and lay down on the hardwood floor.

"Now, Leo," she said, stroking his fur. "It's going to be up to you to take care of Jake when I'm gone."

His purred louder in response.

"Make sure he doesn't work too hard, and he gets

time to surf and swim with you." The cat tilted his head up toward hers, and she kissed him on the nose. "I'm counting on you."

He seemed to nod in response and then yawned. That was good enough for her. She'd better go and scatter the ashes, otherwise, she might miss her flight, and she'd already had a lengthy discussion with the airlines about rebooking the trip she'd been scheduled to take the day they were kidnapped. Apparently, getting abducted wasn't usually cause for a free re-booking, but they'd made an exception for her.

She stood up and picked up the urns. Then she waved a final goodbye to Leo as she stepped through the living room and over to the sliding glass door. Nudging it open with her elbow, she strode out onto the porch. The calm, warm morning breeze coming off of the ocean in the distance enveloped her in its fresh salty scent, and she walked across the patio to the freshly mowed grass that still held some overnight dew. The sun was shining like a bright yellow beacon in the eastern sky, and tiny puffs of fluffy white clouds dotted the cerulean-blue horizon. Her last day in paradise was splendid—a perfect way to say farewell.

She padded off the grass and stepped down the few white wooden steps into the golden glowing sand that was already warmed from the sun. The sheer softness of the sand and the grounding it gave her made tears spring into her eyes. It was stunning here, and it would be hard to say a final goodbye. Not only to her brother and mother but to this place as well. And Jacob. She didn't want to cry any more tears over what had happened and the family she'd lost. She'd gained another one in Jacob, even if he didn't know it. And that, along with her busy life in New York, was enough for her. It had to be.

The waves rolled in a slow and steady motion to the shore and back again in a relaxing rhythm. She'd spent a good part of the last couple of days down here, lounging in the sun and soaking in its healing effects. It had been soul-stirring and tranquil. Just what she needed before she got back to the breakneck pace of the Big Apple.

She shuffled over to a row of surfboards stuck into the sand in an alcove. Jacob kept them close by and available for a quick morning or evening surf. She'd even paddled out on one yesterday and floated in the warm ocean with the sun shining bright on her face until the tide brought her back to shore. Setting down the urns, she selected the colorful blue board she'd used yesterday and heaved it under her arm.

"You weren't thinking of going without me, were you?" A deep masculine voice came from behind her.

She turned to see Jacob standing behind her in green boardshorts and a white rash guard. His short hair was slicked back from his face, and his bright-blue eyes sparkled in the morning sunshine.

She smiled over, and he returned the gesture. My, how she'd miss his warm smile and thoughtfulness. He seemed to know just the right moment to appear. "I thought you were busy working. It's silly, really. I can do it myself."

He shook his head. "You can, but I don't want you to. And neither do your new friends."

Her brow wrinkled in concentration. "New friends?"

"Aloha," Benny called out as he, Grace, and Kai

traipsed down the steps and toward her. Grace wore a red swimsuit, and Benny was dressed in orange swim trunks. Kai rounded out the group in a neon-blue rash guard and matching shorts. They all wore the bright colors of the rainbow, and Grace had her arms full of beautiful white and purple leis.

"We wanted to come," she gushed. "I hope you don't mind. After getting to know who Isaac was through Jake, we feel like we know him too. And you. We want to celebrate his life with you. And lay your mom to rest as well. We do this as a family in Hawaii, and now you're part of our family."

Grace ambled over and enveloped Abby in a warm hug. She returned the gesture and tried to hold back the tears threatening to surface again. Kai and Benny bobbed their agreement, and Kai went over and clasped hands with Grace before taking the leis from her and placing one around her neck with a tenderness Abby had just noticed. Perhaps they were more than friends and colleagues?

When Grace leaned in beside her, Abby whispered, "Is there something going on between you and Kai?"

Grace blushed a deep crimson and shrugged. "It's complicated."

Abby knew all about that. "I get it," she said and left it at that.

She might not ever get the chance to know more about that couple, but she was thankful for their presence. The tears she'd fought back earlier rolled down her cheeks, and she let them this time. "Of course, I want you here. Thank you so much for coming. And thank you for the beautiful flowers."

"It is we who are honored to be here," Kai said as

he made his way over to her and placed the necklace of flowers around her neck. The sweet scent of orchids floated up to her nose, and the coolness of the petals felt good on her warm skin. She hadn't thought of bringing flowers with her to say goodbye, and it was a gesture that touched her heart.

"It's an ancient Hawaiian tradition to have flowers for a sea burial. I'll show you how we do it if you'd like?" Benny offered.

Abby swiped at her tears and smiled back. "Yes. I'd like that."

Once Benny, Grace, and Kai had their leis around their necks, each one of them grabbed a surfboard and headed toward the shore. Jacob came up next to her as she bent down to pick up the urns. "Can I help you carry an urn out to the ocean?"

"Yes." They'd been like brothers, and so it was fitting Jacob would carry Isaac to his final resting place. His treasured ocean.

"Are you all right?" She gazed into his eyes and saw them etched with concern for her. He was in her corner and always had been. It was she who had pushed him away so many years ago. She vowed not to let that happen again despite the miles that would soon separate them.

"I will be. I just need to say goodbye and get going home, y'know?"

He nodded. "You don't have to leave so soon. You can stay here as long as you like. Why not spend a couple more days? Or weeks? I know how much you like it here. You've been kissed by the Hawaiian sun, and you are glowing. You look happy."

She was touched by his generosity and caring. Still,

she shook her head. "I do love it here. It's been wonderful just relaxing these last few days. But I can't stay any longer." If she did, she'd only become more attached to a life that wasn't meant to be for her, and it would break her heart even more than it was breaking right now.

****

Jake was disappointed but not surprised by her answer. He understood. Even if it wasn't what his heart was telling him he wanted. Needed. "I thought you'd say that," he said after a beat. "And I get it."

She smiled over and gave him a shrug. He tried to return the gesture, but it didn't quite reach his eyes. They wadded into the tepid water until it was up to their knees, and then they set down their boards. Abby balanced the urn on the board, then climbed on, chest down. Jake did the same.

The other three were ahead of them. Kai and Grace paddled close to each other while Benny paddled off to the side of them. The lapping of the water as they swept through it with their arms and hands helped Jake breathe a bit easier. The fresh salt smell of the water traveled up to his senses, and he inhaled deeply. This case was taking up all his time. Night and day. But right now, he was where he needed to be. He'd go back to work as soon as Abby was on a plane. A career and his friends would be all he had left after she'd gone.

He was sad to see her go. In the short time she'd been here, he'd gotten used to having her around. Having her in his life. She was someone he could talk to, really talk, and share his day with. She was much more than a friend now, and the passionate night they'd spent together would be forever etched in his memory, but they had different lives. Different worlds. And that was the way it would stay.

They paddled out for another five minutes until Abby stopped and sat up on her board. "This is the place. I want to do it here."

"It's perfect," Jacob agreed, and he slid beside her and positioned his board. Grace was on her other side, and Benny and Kai rounded out the circle in the ocean they had made. The water was quiet out here today and calm. Only a few boats bobbed in the distance.

Jake offered his hand to Abby, and she took it. Maybe for the last time. Her skin was soft and warm, and the sweet scent of coconut floated up to his nose. He wasn't sure he could ever let go. Yet he had to. Benny grabbed his other hand, and their loop was complete. Everyone around him bowed their heads, and Jake did the same.

"Thank you all so much for all being here," Abby said. "It means everything to me that you took the time to paddle out into the ocean as we say goodbye to two lives that touched my heart. And yours."

Jake swiped a tear that had fallen down his cheek as he glanced over at her. She pulled her hand away from his and removed the lid of the urn. Tears rolled down her cheeks as she poured her mother's ashes into the ocean. Jake plunged his hand into the tepid water beside hers and swirled the powder around. Pretty soon, the sea was crystal-clear turquoise again. And now it was his turn to say goodbye to Isaac. His best friend and the buddy he always thought he'd grow old with. But it wasn't meant to be. He bowed his head once again.

Jake unscrewed the cover of the urn and leaned

over to Abby. Together, they poured Isaac's ashes into the warm salty ocean and blended them until they were one with the sea. "*A hui hou,* my friend," Jacob said. "Until we meet again."

Jake nodded over to Kai, who said a prayer in the ancient Hawaiian language. Then he splashed water into the circle, and everyone followed suit until they were drenched and had made waves on the ocean with their movements. Abby laughed, and everyone joined in. Grace took off her lei and threw it into the center of the circle. Benny, Kai, and Abby followed suit, then Jake did it too. The colorful flowers floated on the ocean surface and marked the place where two lives had been laid to rest.

After a beat, Abby looked over at him. "That was beautiful. Thank you."

"*Mahalo,*" Jake responded. "You are most welcome. Are you ready to head back?"

She hesitated, then nodded. "Yes," she said. "It's time for me to go home."

He nodded and then turned his board to paddle back to shore. She was moving on for good.

Without him.

Chapter Sixteen

The rich taste of nutmeg mixed with cinnamon singed his throat as he swallowed. Chai tea was supposed to be a soothing tonic. Meant to relax the soul. But there was nothing that could cure Jake.

The midafternoon sun was high in the sky, and he sat alone on the soft sand in his backyard. Abby was almost ready to board a plane. Back to New York and out of his life. His head told him it was for the best, yet he felt a deep ache in his heart for her tender touch and soothing embrace. She was gone. And she wasn't coming back.

"Here you are!"

A booming voice penetrated the quiet of the afternoon, and Jake looked up with a start. His gaze turned toward the steps to the stand where Benny stood, calm and confident as always, dressed in his uniform and probably coming over from work. Jake knew he should go to work too, there was a lot to do since the governor's arrest, and he just didn't have it today.

"I've been looking all over for you."

He eyed his partner and friend. He wasn't in the mood for Benny's antics. Not today, anyway. "What are you doing here? I told you I'd call you tomorrow."

Benny let out a hearty laugh. "I know, but I just came back to drop off some documents for you to sign and thought I'd check in."

Jake nodded. "Okay. Thanks."

"You okay?"

Jake shook his head. "I don't want to talk about it."

"Of course, you do."

Benny dropped into the sand beside him with a loud thump. He hadn't even taken off his shoes. Jake was barefoot and still in his swim trunks and rash guard from the burial at sea.

"C'mon," Benny urged. "Let's get us some lunch inside, and you can tell me all about it."

"Some other time, huh? It has been a long day. I'm tired." Tired of his life being one train wreck after another. Tired of the possibilities of life, of happiness always slipping through his fingers. And yet here he sat. Doing nothing.

Benny glanced at his watch. "What? It's barely three p.m. Did Abby leave?"

Jake let out a long and heavy breath. "She's at the airport, headed for the mainland. It's over."

Benny raised an eyebrow. "What's over?"

"Abby and me. I mean, it was never really started, but now, it's over. For good." Jake blinked. He hadn't told Benny anything that had happened this past week, and he wasn't about to start now. He didn't want to talk about her. And yet she was all he could think about.

"Buddy. You're not making much sense."

No, he wasn't. And he had a sneaking suspicion he was going to make even less if he continued to talk. Even still.

"I don't know, Benny. Abigail, she's different than any woman I've ever met. Beautiful, kind, caring…" Jake took a swig of his tea and then hissed out a breath. "I kissed her the other night. And then we made love."

Benny's mouth fell open for a split second before he clamped it shut. Then he leaned over and slapped Jake on the shoulder. "Is it serious?"

Jake gave a half shrug. "I wanted it to be. But it didn't work out."

"It didn't work out, or you didn't allow it to work out. Sometimes you're your own worst enemy."

He looked over at his friend, and now it was Benny's turn to shrug. "What's that supposed to mean?"

Benny rolled his eyes. "It means you had feelings for Abby, and you didn't tell her. What if she felt the same? She could be sitting here right now with you instead of your old partner. It would be much more romantic, I'd say."

Benny let out a chuckle, but Jake didn't smile. "She didn't feel the same about me. And I don't blame her. I can't give her what she truly deserves."

Benny cocked his head. "How do you know that for sure? And hey, don't beat yourself up. You've come a long way, man. You should be proud of what you've accomplished."

But what exactly had he accomplished? Gotten a good job and some even better friends? Yet a job couldn't wrap its arms around you and kiss away your bad day. Or hold you in a warm embrace while you fell asleep. He'd been wrong all this time. She was the one for him, but now there was nothing he could do about it. No. Despite all his success, he still felt like a teenager who'd just lost his best friend. Someone who would never find their way. Until Abby came along. And changed things. Changed him.

"How do you know for sure she doesn't feel the

same? Did you even mention it?"

"Not really. But the writing was on the wall." He was out of ideas as to how to solve this problem. He glanced over at Benny, and his smile was wide.

"Want to know what I think?"

He didn't. But his partner would tell him. Whether he liked it or not. He nodded.

"I think you are going to find a way to get past all this." He picked up a handful of sand and let it slide through his fingers.

"How?"

Benny leaned over and grasped his arm. "You deserve someone in your life, someone you haven't let go of. Someone who's still at the airport. Waiting. It's not too late. Not yet at least. You've been given a big chance here. A chance at the life you deserve. Happiness. True love. I can tell you care deeply for Abby. You wouldn't have dropped everything to help her with the case if that weren't so. And if you felt something in that kiss, she probably did too. Don't throw this opportunity away just because you don't want to take another chance. Another risk. Because if you do, the morning will come, and so will regrets."

Benny rose and squeezed his shoulder. "You know what you want. You always have. It's been a long and winding road, but you made it." Benny held out his arm and pointed to the ocean in front of them. "This is your dream come true. But it's missing one piece. Family. And that's by far the most important."

Jake listened to Benny's fading footsteps on the sand until he went up the steps and back into the house. Leaving him with a head full of questions and no definitive answers.

****

"Flight twenty-three fifteen nonstop service to New York City's JFK airport is now boarding." The loudspeaker jolted Abigail out of her daydreaming and back to reality.

She was sitting on a wooden bench in the middle of a bustling terminal, waiting for her flight and marveling at how even the airport in Hawaii seemed different. This section of the terminal where she sat was devoid of windows and instead was open-air, allowing the warm late-afternoon breeze to flow inside. Palm trees swayed in the distance, and the colorful local planes were going in and out. Welcoming passengers to paradise and then escorting them home.

People milled around her with bags and suitcases, but no one was in a hurry like in New York. She took a last deep inhale of the sweet tropical air. She'd bought some pineapples and some coconut candles to take home with her at the gift shop. A little reminder of this idyllic island. She'd miss this place. And she'd miss Jacob even more. Although clearly, it was over.

After they'd paddled back to shore this morning and she'd changed, she said her goodbyes to Grace, Kai, and Benny. After a round of hugs and promises to keep in touch, she and Jacob were left alone. He'd offered an awkward hug and a mumbled goodbye. That had been proof enough to her he didn't feel the same way she felt about him. So she murmured her goodbyes in return and hopped into her rental car, plugging in the GPS coordinates for the airport.

Abigail swung her purse over her shoulder and pulled up the handle on her raspberry-colored suitcase. She strode toward gate sixteen that was crowded with people waiting to board. Just as she was about to join the lineup, she heard a commotion behind her.

"Excuse me, I'm coming through."

She turned to see Jacob dressed in a black HPD polo shirt and khaki pants. He was running toward her with his badge in his hand. His brilliant blue eyes locked on hers, and he skidded to a stop in front of her.

"Abby, you're here." His breath heaved in his chest as if he'd run the entire way from the beach to the airport. She didn't think he had, but she guessed anything was possible with him.

She nodded. "Yes, I am. And now, so are you. What's going on?"

He jerked his head to a quiet corner with a row of blue plastic seats where people had just vacated to get in line. The plane was waiting just outside the window, and people shuffled around them to show their boarding passes and get on the plane.

He turned his gorgeous smile on her. "Can we talk? For just a minute?"

She sighed and glanced at her cell phone in her hand. What more was there to say? She'd said all she had to back at the house, and he'd done the same. Even still.

"A minute is about all I've got. My flight is boarding. I'm in line."

He nodded. "I know. This will only take a minute, and then if you still want to get on this plane, I'll make sure you do."

She let out a long breath. If she didn't let him say his piece, she'd forever wonder what he wanted to tell her. "Okay, fine. But only one minute. I am not rebooking this flight again."

He nodded, and she hitched her purse higher on her shoulder as she excused herself about fifty times to get around the line of brightly colored and suntanned tourists and followed him over to the window where he was now standing. What in the world was going on? He wore a serious expression, and they'd already said their goodbyes. Did this have something to do with the case?

"Is everything all right?" She moved her hands to reach out to him but stopped herself. It would only cause her more heartache if she did that. Instead, she set down her suitcase and bags, then crossed her arms in front of her chest.

He shook his head. "No. It's not all right."

She felt her forehead crinkle in concentration. "What is it? What do you need?"

A shy smile curved his lips. "What I need Abigail is you."

****

He was doing this all wrong. Clearly, rehearsing with Benny all the way over here with sirens blazing in the HPD uniformed car had been an epic waste of time. Partially because Benny wouldn't stop laughing at him, but mostly because Jake had forgotten everything he'd wanted to say to her. Everything. Except for the way she made him feel.

She'd only been gone a few hours, and yet he'd missed her so much it was a physical pain deep inside his gut that hadn't abated till he'd laid eyes on her moments ago. He'd missed the feeling of her smooth skin on his. Missed her light voice and tender gaze. Missed the fact that after all that had been said and done, she still cared. How could he have let her go?

Her wide eyes and open mouth mixed with a hint

of a frown told him he was about to lose her again if he didn't start talking.

"Jake, what are you saying?"

It wasn't so much what he had to say. It was what he had to do.

He shuffled his feet and then pulled a small black velvet box from his pocket. Then he dropped to one knee and held it up. Her hand flew to her chest, and her breath heaved.

"When I imagined doing this, it wasn't here. In amongst a crowded airport with everyone staring at us." He motioned to the crowd who had stopped boarding to gawk at them. Women wearing bright colored dresses clutched their chests, and men in Hawaiian shirts gave them the thumbs-up sign.

"I imagined a candlelight dinner on the beach with flowers and fancy silverware. All of the things you deserve. But after you left, I wasn't sure you felt the same way about me as I did about you. Then I realized I need to take another chance. A chance on love. I couldn't wait a moment longer to ask you the question I've been thinking about ever since we kissed."

Jake pried open the box in his palm and held it out to her. She gasped, and her eyes danced in bright sunshine streaming in through the window. A stunning white gold band sat nestled in among the black velvet. It had a smattering of diamonds made into the shape of a flower that now reminded him of her. She was the flower that had opened up his heart. To freedom, and to love. It had been the one thing he'd managed to save of his mother's, and now he wanted her to have it.

"When you showed up at my place, you were the last person I wanted to see. I was determined to erase everything and everyone in my past. And even though we've only spent a short time together since you've gotten here, you haven't been far from my mind. I know I'm not perfect. Far from it. But my love for you is strong. Stronger than anything I've ever felt before."

He cleared his throat before he continued. The hardest part was yet to come. But she needed to know the truth. All of it. He needed to say it out loud. Then the forgiveness would be real. The healing would begin. And he'd start his new life. The one that mattered. Her expression was upturned, and a small smile graced her beautiful features. It spurred him on.

"My love for you was strong enough to push me out of my shell and love again despite everything we've both been through. Now I can finally admit to myself what I've known all along. You are my one and only true soulmate. I need to take another chance on love. Another chance on love with you. I want to grow old with you. I want to love you forever and always. Abigail Hastings, will you marry me?"

****

Emotions welled up in Abby and then overflowed. As in the gushing rapids of Niagara Falls overflowing. All her buried hopes and dreams were coming to pass. There was a happily ever after. A happily ever after for her and Jake. They belonged together. The family she'd been searching for had been right in front of her entire time.

She launched herself into his arms, and he caught her and pulled her into him. The hard planes of his chest melded against her, and she reveled in the feeling of being held again by the man she loved. This time, for good.

"Yes, Jake Devereaux. I love you. With all my heart and soul. And marrying you will make us the family we are meant to be." Tears streamed down her cheeks, and he kissed them away with his tender lips.

Once her tears washed away, his lips met hers. Tentative at first. She opened up to him, and he kissed her. Long and deep. His tongue sought hers, and they entwined as if they'd never been apart. He smelled of sea salt and bergamot. She inhaled deeply.

Her heart slowed as he held and kissed her. And touched her soul. After she broke the kiss, in order to catch her breath, she leaned back and looked at him. Cheers rose up in the small audience beside them. Abby and Jake waved at them, and they cheered some more. Then she turned back. "But what changed? Why now?"

He shook his head. "Not what. But who? It was me. I changed. My life was empty before you came along. Oh sure, I had a good job, but what I didn't realize was none of that matters without love. It made me whole. Complete. I couldn't see the forest for the trees until you came along. Family is what matters. And my family won't be complete without you."

"Neither will mine. You are my family. And you always will be. I should have realized that sooner. But I do now, and that's all that matters." Her heart swelled with happiness. She had started this trip to solve her brother's murder. But along the way, she fell in love. Madly. Truly. Deeply. And found the family her heart desired.

"So I guess I'm not making this flight, huh?" She smiled and pulled him in for another kiss.

He indulged her, then leaned back and gazed at her, shaking his head. "No way. You don't need a flight to

New York. Now, or ever unless you want to."

"Right now, this is exactly where I want to be." She laughed. "Well, maybe at your cottage would be better, but I'm not leaving the island."

"I was hoping you'd say that."

He pulled her back into his embrace for another kiss and took her hand. He slid the elegant white gold band on her finger, and she wasn't surprised when it was a perfect fit.

Epilogue

Six Months Later

"Are you ready? This is it, Jake. There's no turning back now." Benny laughed a little too loudly for the current venue and slapped him on the shoulder. Even on his wedding day, he wasn't spared his friends' antics. But he wouldn't want it any other way.

They stood inside at the end of the aisle in a century-old church nestled on the beach in Honolulu. Dressed in a white Hawaiian shirt and khakis, Jake waited, rather impatiently, for the ceremony to begin. The place wasn't full, but quite a few people turned out in the antique wood pews to wish the couple well. Both the front and back doors to the church were wide open, and a cool breeze blew through it, carrying a refreshing salty scent. Out in the back of the church, a makeshift dance floor and white linen-covered tables had been set up. After the service, this was where they'd celebrate their marriage with a proper Hawaiian luau.

Abby, now a resident of Hawaii, worked for the local paper, *The Honolulu Star*. She reported on feel-good stories from around the island and had recently had a work of fiction published. She'd invited some of her new friends from the paper to celebrate with them. And half of the HPD was in attendance after Benny gave out invitations without consulting Jake.

Large stained-glass windows with elaborate bible scenes gave off a soft, calming light and comforted him. It wasn't that he was nervous, per se. And he'd never in a million years admit that to Benny. It was just that he wanted everything to be perfect for his gorgeous bride on this special day. And since she'd wanted a traditional church wedding complete with her new extended family and friends, here they were. The most important ones to him were Benny beside him and Grace along with Kai in the second row. They wore traditional Hawaiian outfits and waved over at him.

He waved back and surveyed the space. A team of decorators had spun silk tulle ribbons with boughs of hibiscus and palms at the end of each aisle. Huge bouquets of the same flowers mixed with vine cuttings flagged the entrance.

Jake took a deep breath, and the sweet scent helped him to imagine their upcoming honeymoon. Tucked away in their cottage at the beach. Just the two of them for an entire week. Jake nodded and smiled over at Benny. "I'm ready. I've been waiting for this for a long time. But you know what I can't wait for?"

"What's that?" Benny wrinkled his forehead.

"Your turn."

Benny scoffed. "No way, man. I'm staying single. For life."

Jake winked. "We'll see."

The wedding march started up on the organ. The sweet music floated up to his ears, and he felt his heartbeat relax just a little. He stood up straight and gazed at the vision in ivory standing just outside the entrance to the church.

Abby wore a veil that cascaded down her to her

waist. Her long ebony hair peek out beneath the silk tulle, and his heart melted at the sight of her. Her satin strapless empire-waist gown with a Hawaiian design down one side made her look like a princess. His Hawaiian princess. She was by far the most beautiful creature he had ever laid eyes on.

She held a small bouquet consisting of two hibiscus flowers—one to represent her mother and one to represent her brother. Leo the cat trailed behind her like he was the star of the show today, and Jake smiled as the three of them were about to become a family.

She floated toward him to the beat of the organ. The congregation stood up as she walked by each pew. Jake smiled and strode down the two carpeted steps to meet her. He peeled back the veil to reveal his blushing bride. "You look beautiful," he whispered in her ear. "I can't wait to marry you."

She gazed up at him with those wide dark eyes that had captivated him from the moment he'd laid eyes on her at his cottage. The day his life changed. For the better. Forever.

"I love you, too, but I'm not your wife yet. You still need to make an honest woman out of me."

He chuckled and leaned down to kiss her cheek. The sweet scent of coconut enveloped him. "No. It's you who made an honest man out of me. Today and every day for the rest of our lives, your wish is my command."

She smiled and took his hand in hers. Then they walked up the steps to the front of the church and the waiting minister. Where they would become husband and wife. And live happily ever after in paradise.

A word about the author…

After writing more essays than she could count completing her university studies, Kate Randle decided to swap out the world of academic prose for something more exciting, romance novels.

She lives near Toronto, Ontario, although she loves to travel anywhere with a beach, and these settings frequently make it into her books. Her incredibly supportive husband and two kids along with five rescue felines round out her family to keep things interesting and covered in cat hair.